O Beautiful

Theresa Rebeck

A SAMUEL FRENCH ACTING EDITION

SAMUEL FRENCH

FOUNDED 1830

SAMUELFRENCH.COM
SAMUELFRENCH-LONDON.CO.UK

O BEAUTIFUL was commissioned and first produced by the Resident Ensemble Players (REP) of the University of Delaware (Sanford Robbins, Producing Artistic Director) in Newark, Delaware on April 22, 2011. The performance was directed by Sanford Robbins, with sets by Takeshi Kata, costumes by Martha Hally, lights by Chris Akerlind, sound design and compositions by Fitz Patton and Alex Neumann, and projections by Eileen Smitheimer. The Production Stage Manager was Rick Cunningham. The cast was as follows:

ALICE FLETCHER . . . . Sarah Griffin

JESUS . . . . Michael Gotch

TY JANALERIS . . . . Donte Fitzgerald

ERIK WATERS . . . . Erik Mathew

LUKE SIMPSON . . . . Matthew Simpson

GWEN TURNER . . . . Meaghan Sullivan

LENNIE RYAN . . . . Ben Charles

SIMON WEST . . . . Mic Matarrese

PATRICK HENRY/DON FLETCHER . . . . Andy Nagraj

LINDA RYAN . . . . Elizabeth Heflin

BRIAN RYAN/ALEXANDER HAMILTON . . . . Matt Loney

MRS. LOOMIS . . . . Kathleen Pirkl Tague

MARCIA TURNER . . . . Caroline Crocker

BRENDA WATERS . . . . Carine Montbertrand

ARLENE FLETCHER . . . . Deena Burke

JOE SIMPSON/THOMAS JEFFERSON . . . . Steve Tague

SONDRA JANALERIS . . . . Jasmine Bracey

MINISTER/JOHN ADAMS . . . . Andrew Goldwasser

SAINT PAUI/BENJAMIN FRANKLIN . . . . Drew Brhel

SAINT DENIS . . . . Andrew Goldwasser, Annie Hudson

JOAN OF ARC . . . . Caroline Crocker

OTHER PARENTS, TEACHERS, AND STUDENTS . Carolynn Ashoff, Chloe Berk, Jennifer Carter, Anique Clements, Colleen Cordaro, Andrew Corddry, August DiAmato, Marisa Dashaies, Matt Deis, Mary-Elizabeth Dina, Zachary Dupras, Andrew Goldwasser, Kyle Gordon, Annie Hudson, Lisle Hummerston, Adeel Arsalan Iqbal, Amanda Mouser, Tony Qian, Tim Saunders, Brian Tighe, Sarah Truitt, Mike Wilson, and Inyong Yea

CHARACTERS

ALICE FLETCHER

JESUS

TY JANALERIS

ERIK WATERS

LUKE SIMPSON

GWEN TURNER

LENNIE RYAN

SIMON WEST

PATRICK HENRY / DON FLETCHER

LINDA RYAN

BRIAN RYAN / ALEXANDER HAMILTON

MRS. LOOMIS

MARCIA TURNER

BRENDA WATERS

ARLENE FLETCHER

JOE SIMPSON / THOMAS JEFFERSON

SONDRA JANALERIS

MINISTER / JOHN ADAMS

ST. PAUL / BENJAMIN FRANKLIN

ST. DENIS

JOAN OF ARC

OTHER PARENTS, TEACHERS, AND STUDENTS

SETTING

A high school gymnasium, homes, classrooms,
a TV soundstage, limbo

TIME

Present Day

ACT ONE

*(A bare stage. **ALICE** alone with **JESUS**.)*

ALICE. I'm just real confused.

JESUS. I know.

ALICE. I don't feel any different.

JESUS. I know!

ALICE. But I'm like totally different, now, aren't I?

JESUS. I don't know.

ALICE. There's me and like this other person. But I don't feel like there's this other person.

JESUS. I know.

ALICE. I mean we were just making out and all of a sudden he's like, taking his pants off. It was like in the back of his stupid car.

JESUS. In the back of his *car*?

ALICE. Yes! He was all, God, I can't even, it's even not such a great car. Like it's a *Honda*, it was his uncle's Honda, and his dad bought it for him and it's brown. Like who drives a brown car? And the upholstery is it's not even leather it's that sort of fabric that you don't even know what it is, is it real, even, and it was pink, pink and maroon, and I was I KNEW he was going to try something why on earth would you say 'let's check out the back seat?' Like is there something *in*teresting back there, in the back seat? The icky upholstery? And I did, I said NO, I said no God please I don't want to but he just kept going and I tried to push him off but he just kept, he kept –

JESUS. Wow.

ALICE. I can't have a baby! My parents will kill me, my dad will kill me. And I don't understand like why should I have a baby? Why doesn't the guy who stuck his penis in me have the stupid baby, he's the one who made this happen.

JESUS. It just doesn't work that way.

ALICE. That's not my fault! I mean okay I'm an idiot, but does that mean I have to have a baby? Whose idea was that?

JESUS. You're not an idiot.

ALICE. Don't be nice about this!

JESUS. I'm just trying to listen.

ALICE. *(screams in frustration)* Okay okay, but this is my point. I read the new testament, I read the whole thing, my whole life I've read the whole thing! And you never say anything about abortion! You never say, nobody's ever allowed to have an abortion ever.

JESUS. No, I didn't.

ALICE. If it's so fucking important why didn't you even mention it? You're Jesus, right?

JESUS. Yeah!

ALICE. I mean the actual Jesus, we're not kidding around. You're Jesus.

JESUS. Yes, I'm Jesus.

ALICE. And you didn't. Did you ever say, 'I'm Jesus and I say that stupid girls who let guys talk them into going to the back seat of their cars have to have babies?' Did you say that ever?

JESUS. No.

ALICE. All you talk about is be nice to each other! You never said nobody's allowed to have an abortion.

JESUS. No.

ALICE. So can I? Can I? Can I?

(A beat.)

JESUS. Honesty, I – I don't really have an issue with it.

(Blackout)

(**TY** *teaching a class. He reads from a paper in his hand.*)

TY. The historian's distortion is more than technical, it is ideological; it is released into a world of contending interests. Let's look at the first two words. Historian's distortion. What's that? Mr. Waters.

ERIK. I don't…what was the question?

(*His friends snicker.*)

TY. Mr. Zinn, the author of today's essay, uses the phrase "historian's distortion," I'd like you to try and explain to the class what that means.

ERIK. I don't know, I didn't say it.

TY. What does it mean to you?

ERIK. What does what mean?

TY. Are we not speaking the same language, Mr. Waters?

ERIK. I guess not.

TY. Miss Fletcher, would you like to give it a try?

ALICE. No thank you.

TY. Come on people the world is coming to an end and you all are the generation that is going to have to decide if you're going to let that happen. We need some critical thinking here!

LUKE. If the world is coming to an end how come we have to study history?

(**ERIK** *snickers.*)

TY. That actually is a halfway sensible question. Anybody want to take it on? Mr. Ryan?

LENNIE. I guess, I don't know. It doesn't have to come to an end, does it?

LUKE. The Bible says it does.

GWEN. We're not allowed to talk about the Bible, it's a public school, remember?

TY. Let's go back to this idea of historical distortion. What does it mean? Mr. Simpson.

LUKE. I don't know!

TY. Guess. Mr. Ryan.

LENNIE. Well, I think it means, somebody, there's somebody in history who had this idea and it was an okay idea a long time ago but it's not as good an idea anymore and we still believe it.

TY. Yes!

GWEN. This is American history. Aren't we supposed to be talking about America?

*(Lights shift. **SIMON WEST** is on television. As he speaks, **LINDA** watches. She is making dinner. After a moment, **LENNIE** joins her. He sits at the kitchen table and does homework.)*

SIMON. We are under seige, ladies and gentlemen. Our way of life has come under the most insidious of threats, not from outside forces which are gathering beyond our shores with nefarious purposes, those evil people are there, I'm not saying they aren't, we've seen already how serious they are in their intent to destroy America and all it stands for. I'm not saying the Godless jihadist has laid down his weapon and come to love and appreciate the democracy and freedom our great nation offers the world, the beacon we hold up is there, but they cannot tolerate the light, like poor demented vampires whose hunger feeds on darkness, they shrink from the sunshine of truth, they shrink from America. But they want to destroy us too. And we confront them, we do, with courage and strength, and – I'm sorry – my strength is failing, I can't, I can't – can someone get me a glass of water, can –

*(A **PRODUCTION ASSISTANT** appears with a glass of water and hands it to him.)*

Thank you thank you, I feel – so weak, I can't – but I can't drink this! It's polluted! It's muddy, it's, food, food, I need food –

(He pushes the glass of water away. Another **PRODUCTION ASSISTANT** *appears with a plate of food.)*

Thank you, thank you, I don't know what has happened, I feel so weak, I need sustenance –

(off food)

But what's this? This is, this food is spoiled. The meat, it's gone bad, it's inedible, it's –

(He pushes it away.)

my strength is gone – I need a weapon, something to use, to defend myself against mine enemies, where is my weapon?

(Another **PRODUCTION ASSISTANT** *runs in and offers him a big semi-automatic rifle.)*

Thank you, thank you, I'm so weak – but now I'm strong.

(He cuts the weak act and holds up the gun.)

We are being poisoned from within. Our very government is poisoning America, poisoning our food and our water so that when our enemies arrive on our shores, the only strength we have left will be this.

(He holds up his weapon.)

But make no mistake, my friends. Our weapons are powerful. And they have saved us before. We will destroy our enemies with steel and fire as we were told, by our founding fathers.

LINDA. *(laughing)* Oh he's just awful.

LENNIE. Why do you watch him?

LINDA. Your father likes him.

LENNIE. Dad's not here.

LINDA. Just a habit.

SIMON. We have a special guest tonight.

LINDA. How was school today?

LENNIE. Okay.

SIMON. Someone who knows a few things about the fight against tyranny.

LENNIE. A little boring.

LINDA. How'd your audition go?

SIMON. A man who can speak from experience about getting the job done.

LENNIE. I didn't do it.

SIMON. Mr. Patrick Henry!

LINDA. Why not?

LENNIE. I didn't want to.

PATRICK HENRY. *(acknowledging applause)* Thank you. Thank you, citizens.

LINDA. I think you do, sweetheart. I know you do.

PATRICK HENRY. They tell us, sir, that we are weak.

SIMON. I know they do!

PATRICK HENRY. Unable to cope with so formidable an adversary. But when will we be stronger?

LENNIE. It's just a stupid talent show.

PATRICK HENRY. Will it be next week, or next year?

LINDA. You love that show! You go every year.

PATRICK HENRY. Will it be when we are totally disarmed?

LENNIE. It's for nerds, Mom.

PATRICK HENRY. And when a British guard shall be stationed in every house?

LINDA. It's for talented young people! That's why they call it a talent show.

PATRICK HENRY. It is in vain, sir, to extenuate the matter.

LENNIE. I don't want to!

LINDA. Oh sweetheart.

PATRICK HENRY. Gentlemen may cry peace, peace, but there is no peace. The war is actually begun! The next gale that sweeps from the north will bring to our ears the clash of resounding arms! Forbid it, almighty god! I know not what course others may take, but as for me, give me liberty or give me death!

(Loud applause. **LINDA** *and* **LENNIE** *turn their attention to the show.)*

LENNIE. I wonder where they got that guy.

LINDA. Who knows.

*(***SIMON*** puts his arm around* **PATRICK HENRY.***)*

SIMON. You've just heard from a true American hero. A defender of this nation from a time before we were a nation. And he's speaking to you now.

(A **PRODUCTION ASSISTANT** *gives him and* **SIMON** *assault rifles. They hold them together.)*

SIMON. Because the time is now.

(More thunderous applause. The two men wave their rifles in the light.)

BRIAN. *(off)* I'm home!

LINDA. Oh hi honey! We're in the kitchen!

(to **LENNIE***)*

Well, I really think you'll be missing out if you don't even try.

LENNIE. What's for dinner?

LINDA. Oh I'm making that chicken and rice cassarole you like. Three cans of soup! Cream of mushroom, cream of chicken and cream of celery. I know it's a little rich but my goodness it's – what on earth. WHAT ON EARTH.

*(***BRIAN*** enters. He carries an assault rifle.)*

BRIAN. I bought a gun.

*(***LINDA*** drops her can of soup. They go. The principal,* **MRS. LOOMIS,** *confronts* **TY.***)*

TY. It was a handout. It's supplemental reading.

MRS LOOMIS. Yes, that's I think what people are concerned about, that it is not considered an approved text.

TY. Nowhere does it say that handouts, supplemental material has always been considered an acceptable.

MRS LOOMIS. *(overlap)* School policy as stated leaves no room whatsoever for interpretation.

TY. *(overlap)* – Teaching tool, I use it as a supplement to the text that the state dictates.

MRS LOOMIS. You're getting a little heated, Mr. Janaleris.

TY. I am not heated, I am just concerned.

MRS LOOMIS. It's a public school, Ty. The public gets a voice.

TY. I am aware.

MRS LOOMIS. When I was teaching I never felt the need for supplemental reading. My text books were all ancient. I mean, really just falling apart but I stuck to the readings in the text.

TY. I use my textbook.

MRS LOOMIS. But you're teaching other things too.

TY. I'm teaching them how to think. I hope you're not saying I shouldn't be teaching them that.

MRS LOOMIS. Well, some of the parents expressed concern. As I think you knew they would.

TY. Who.

MRS LOOMIS. It doesn't matter who the complaint came from, as I think you well know. Once the school board chooses to involve itself.

TY. It was a handout!

MRS LOOMIS. Are we suggesting we let the school board take a vote? Whether or not the school should ban handouts.

TY. Are you suggesting we censor ourselves and not even wait for the school board to do it?

(A beat.)

MRS LOOMIS. I would hate it if it got back to the teachers union that I said anything like "censor." I'm just presenting the hope that we will all be circumspect with the materials we choose.

(She is finished. They go.)

*(**LUKE, GWEN** and **ERIK**. They are hanging out, and texting on their cell phones.)*

LUKE. Bitch!

GWEN. Fuck you.

LUKE. Fuck you too.

*(They continue texting. **ERIK** laughs at something he sees on his cell.)*

ERIK. Oh shit! That is, you're a fucking perv.

LUKE. You're a perv. Like dude, you have got to get yourself a a hobby or a girl or read a book or something. A mind is a terrible thing to waste.

(He texts him.)

ERIK. Shit! Stop it! That is like fucking illegal man you are a serious asshole.

*(He is laughing at his cell phone. **LUKE** looks up from his at **GWEN**.)*

LUKE. Seriously? You would do that? For me?

*(**GWEN** laughs at him. They kiss. **ERIK** ignores them making out, while he continues texting. **ALICE** enters, with **JESUS**, sees them. She balks, starts to turn around.)*

JESUS. Wait wait wait.

ALICE. Jesus, stop it. No. Jesus. Please.

JESUS. You have to do it.

ALICE. I can't talk to him while he's – he's –

*(She makes a sound of horrified frustration and leaves. **JESUS** follows her off. After a moment, he comes back on, leading **ALICE** by the hand. She is reluctant but he pushes her, gently toward the others. **ERIK** elbows **LUKE**.)*

ERIK. Dude.

*(**LUKE** looks up, sees **ALICE**.)*

LUKE. Hey.

ALICE. Hi. Um, can I, I have to talk to you.

LUKE. So talk.

ALICE. Alone. Actually, could I talk to you alone?

(ERIK *reacts.* GWEN *looks up at* ALICE, *offended.*)

GWEN. Hello excuse me.

ERIK. Whooooa.

GWEN. Mind your business, asshole. And you mind yours too, bitch.

ERIK. *(laughing)* Whoa!

GWEN. You just show up and say I have to leave, I don't think so. I really do not fucking think so.

ALICE. I'll come back.

GWEN. I don't think you will.

JESUS. Dude why are you letting this girl get all in your business? Does she thinks she has rights or something? What the fuck? I mean, I don't mean what the fuck, that's not good language and you should be more careful with your words, using words with respect but I also don't think you should just sit there and let this female think she has some sort of rights, to tell you who you can or cannot talk to! I mean it, dude. God is love, and you got to love everybody that includes this young girl here, who look, you got to admit, you really do need to be decent to her and I'm going to be discreet and not mention why.

LUKE. Who are you?

JESUS. I'm Jesus, man. Come on. I'm Jesus. And I'm telling you. You got to be decent and at least have the conversation.

LUKE. Okay. You're right. It's okay.

GWEN. It's not okay!

LUKE. I said it's okay, Gwen! You're not allowed to tell me who I talk to!

GWEN. Screw you.

(*She stands and goes, in a huff.* LUKE *tips his head at* ERIK *who, laughing, goes.* ALICE *and* LUKE *and* JESUS *are alone.*)

LUKE. So, what?

ALICE. I…

LUKE. Look, you didn't tell anybody about what happened, right? Like, I like you, but that was kind of a one time situation, you know that, right? 'Cause me and Gwen, you know.

ALICE. Sure.

LUKE. So are we cool?

(*She stares at him, silent.* **JESUS** *elbows her.*)

ALICE. (*blurting*) I'm pregnant.

LUKE. What?

ALICE. I'm pregnant. I'm pregnant.

LUKE. Oh, Christ.

JESUS. No, it's true, man.

LUKE. Well, what do you expect me to do about it? That was a one time thing. Did I not just say, that was a one time thing? I mean, I'm not going to marry you!

ALICE. I don't want to marry you.

LUKE. Well, what do you want?

ALICE. I want an abortion.

LUKE. (*appalled*) What?

ALICE. I just don't want, I don't want this either!

LUKE. So what, you want to kill it? That's what you want to do, you just want to kill it?

ALICE. I need –

LUKE. Abortion is a sin. It's murder! You want to murder a baby? That's disgusting.

JESUS. Dude, maybe you should dial it down.

LUKE. Are you all right with this?

JESUS. I'm just trying to have compassion, man.

LUKE. You can't have compassion for killers!

ALICE. I said NO! I SAID NO and you kept ugh, and you didn't, you didn't even pretend to use a condom! I said NO. YOU did this, I said NO –

LUKE. Would you keep it down? Christ, you sound crazy you know that?

ALICE. THAT'S WHAT HAPPENED.

LUKE. What happened is you wanted it and you got it. You kill this baby, that's on you.

(He goes. **ALICE** *waits for a moment, then goes in the opposite direction.)*

*(***LINDA*** *is setting up a bake sale with* **BRENDA** *and* **MARCIA**.)*

MARCIA. Oh good I was hoping you'd make your cream cheese brownies.

LINDA. Well I know how much you like them.

MARCIA. I do but my hips don't!

BRENDA. Oh I left the cupcakes in the car.

LINDA. *(startled)* You did cupcakes, too?

BRENDA. Everybody always likes the cupcakes, they sell so well.

(She goes.)

LINDA. My goodness we've got a LOT of cupcakes. Louise is bringing six dozen, because she said the same thing.

MARCIA. Well, if there's too much we can always take them home.

LINDA. Oh you made those rice crispie treats that look like mice, I love how you do that. It seems like such a shame to let all those teenagers just eat them.

MARCIA. I almost didn't make anything at all, I'm so mad at the school right now.

LINDA. Really? Why?

(She looks around, making sure no one can hear.)

MARCIA. Oh, all these things they're teaching. Gwen came home last week with all this extra reading. You know what the extra reading was? All about history isn't history. It's all made up.

*(***BRENDA*** *re-enters with cupcakes.)*

BRENDA. I heard about this.

LINDA. I didn't

(**ARLENE** *enters, carrying cookies.*)

ARLENE. Sorry, sorry, my prayer group went late.

BRENDA. People needed extra prayers today?

LINDA. We can all use a few extra prayers.

(**LINDA** *puts up a sign.*)

BRENDA. What did we decide? A dollar for the cupcakes –

LINDA. A dollar for everything.

ARLENE. You can't charge a dollar for the cookies, they're not big enough.

LINDA. A dollar for two.

ARLENE. So fifty cents for one?

LINDA. We were trying to not have to make a lot of change.

BRENDA. Did you hear in New York they're not allowed to have bake sales anymore?

LINDA. No bake sales. You have to be kidding me.

BRENDA. You're not allowed to sell anything with sugar in it, on school property.

LINDA. That's ridiculous.

BRENDA. No they're doing it someplace else, too –

ARLENE. Pennsylvania. I saw it too. It was on the news.

BRENDA. Hey, you see Simon West last week, he had Patrick Henry on? It was hilarious.

BRENDA. I saw that.

LINDA. I saw it too and it scared me. All that talk about guns.

BRENDA. It is a constitutional right.

LINDA. Yeah, but…

MARCIA. You don't have a gun in your house? Ed has like six.

LINDA. Six?

MARCIA. I think it's six. Five or six. No wait! Yeah it is, it's six.

(They go.)

(The talent show. Everyone gathers to watch.)

TY. Hello. Hi! Hello, welcome, welcome to the annual Selbyville High Talent Spectacular. This is my first year here at Selbyville, for those who don't know me, my name is Mr. Janilaris, I'm the new American history teacher and I also teach civics to the incoming freshmen. Anyway I'm really pleased to be participating here, tonight, as your emcee for this terrific event, we have a long line of musical acts and a couple of comedy sketches lined up as well, so let's get to it! On with the show! First up, sophomore Leonard Ryan has volunteered to start tonight's festivities with an invocation of the American ideals which we hope are present for all of us, any time we come together as a community. Leonard?

*(***LENNIE*** goes to the microphone, nervous. All watch as he takes a breath and then sings, acapella.)*

LENNIE. O beautiful, for spacious skies, for amber waves of grain, for purple mountains – travesty, above the fruited plain!

(He is less and less sure of himself.)

Amerrrica, Amerrrrica, god spread his face on me, and crown my good with motherhood, um, be oh let it be!!

*(He cringes. ***LINDA*** stands, clapping.)*

*(The others leave. ***LINDA*** and ***LENNIE*** at home.)*

LINDA. You were terrific!

LENNIE. I was horrible, Mom!

LINDA. You weren't, honey –

LENNIE. I couldn't remember the words! I sang the words wrong!

LINDA. Nobody noticed.

LENNIE. How could you not notice! I was first! I was first!

LINDA. And nobody else was as good, I thought.

LENNIE. You think that because you're my mom!

LINDA. Oh, everybody thinks that we don't know anything because we're just the moms, she's just mom she doesn't know anything.

LENNIE. You DON'T know anything!

LINDA. I know you're perfect.

LENNIE. That wasn't perfect!

LINDA. No, it wasn't. But it was funny and and brave and I don't know. Human.

LENNIE. I'm in high school! Nothing is supposed to be human! Oh god. I sucked.

LINDA. I wish you could see yourself the way I see you. I thought you were fantastic. I thought you were the best one.

(GWEN, LUKE and ERIK enter with cell phones.)

GWEN. You suck.

ERIK. You think you're talented? That's why you tried out for the talent show?

LUKE. That fucking talent show is for pussies.

ERIK. That talent show is a travesty.

LUKE. Above the fruited plain.

GWEN. He didn't even know the words to the song!

ERIK. You like fruit? Oh wait maybe you are a fruit.

LUKE. You like fruit, fruit?

GWEN. Fucking fag.

LUKE. Pussy.

(DON, BRIAN and JOE, having beers. LUKE has a magazine.)

JOE. Look at this. German machine gun. Fires four hundred and fifty rounds a minute accurate up to a range of eighteen hundred meters.

DON. What's that in feet?

BRIAN. Multiply by three.

JOE. That's about five thousand feet. Plus change.

BRIAN. That can't be right.

JOE. It's what it says.

DON. That thing fires 450 rounds a minute? Accurate up to a mile?

BRIAN. I don't believe it.

JOE. Killed hundreds of thousands of troops during the war.

DON. Which war is this?

JOE. German machine gun, it would have to be World War II. Last great war.

BRIAN. Somebody's selling that?

JOE. Gun show up in Williamsport.

(He shows him the ad.)

BRIAN. Boy that's something.

(He looks at it.)

JOE. You're not looking to expand already are you? That beauty you picked up last month is a gorgeous weapon. This is more an antique. It's not going to do anything your piece won't cover.

BRIAN. Oh no no I'm real happy with what I got. The wife's less than thrilled. But you're not hearing any complaints from me.

JOE. Linda's not happy?

BRIAN. No, it's nothing. You know. Guns make women nervous.

DON. Arlene's fine with it!

JOE. It's about protection. I don't see why a woman would object to that.

BRIAN. I didn't mean, Linda's fine, she just, it made her nervous to have it, you know. Right in the house. It's a pretty intimidating weapon, first time you see it.

JOE. Anytime you see it.

BRIAN. That's what I mean. She just felt like it would be safer, to keep it in a lockbox, out in the garage.

JOE. How is that safer? It's totally inaccessible out there.

BRIAN. No, no, the garage is right off the kitchen. I think she's right. This kind of weaponry, it's more for professional situations.

DON. So what are you doing for your personal safety?

BRIAN. What do you mean?

DON. In the house, what are you doing for your personal safety in the house. If your Heckler's out in the garage –

BRIAN. Oh yeah yeah yeah, well I'll take care of that in time.

JOE. In time for what?

BRIAN. I'm just saying this is new to her and me as well. Me as well!

JOE. If it's new that's only because you've hidden the necessity of it in your mind, till now.

BRIAN. No doubt.

JOE. I know there are skeptics.

BRIAN. I'm not skeptical.

DON. But Linda.

BRIAN. What about her?

DON. She's skeptical. Arlene already told me, she's telling everybody. She's got a problem.

JOE. It's a free country, people are allowed to hold that opinion. But just because others want to blind themselves to the danger of these times, doesn't mean we do. You buy a gun, you can't be afraid of it. You buy a gun and you're not ready to use it? What happens when you need to use it? The moment of necessity, when someone is coming at you, someone is entering your home against your will, there is no room for hesitation or fear in that moment. You need to reach for your weapon and use it. You can't think of your weapon as something that's safe. What use to you is it, if it's safe? It's as useless as your brain, telling you over and over again, I just want to be safe. Wanting to be safe is what puts you in danger.

(He takes the magazine and starts to flip through it.)

JOE. She's a good woman. There is no question, your wife is a good woman, and her fears are reasonable. You don't need to deny them. But you can't be ruled by them, either.

(He shoves the magazine over to **BRIAN**. **BRIAN** *looks at it.)*

*(***LENNIE**, *alone.)*

LENNIE. This is what I don't understand: why things come out of your mouth that you don't know why they're coming out of your mouth. Like, there's a person inside you, right, who's in charge. If that person isn't you then who is that person? And who is the one who thinks things like 'Oh I'll just do this stupid thing and that will be fine.' Like, O Beautiful – like you think I'll sing this song, and it will be scary but kind of cool, a cool good thing to do. Honestly, like right now when I even just talk about it, it seems like such a stupid idea, such a collosally, who would ever think that that was a good idea? In what universe? And then when the words that come out aren't even the right words, it's like whose idea was this and who is the person in here making up these words? In front of – you know, the whole – I mean it's like this: People say, high school sucks. And that sort of is supposed to make it okay, because everybody knows it sucks. And then you think when people say that, what they think they mean is that high school sucks but the rest of life is going to be okay. Isn't that what that means? But then you look around and go high school doesn't actually suck for everyone, why can't I be one of the people it doesn't suck for?

Because sometimes when I'm doing my homework – or I look around and there's a person who's – and you think wow, this could be great. But maybe knowing that is sort of like knowing the words to O Beautiful.

I mean the fact is maybe you don't, maybe you don't know them at all.

(TY passing out another handout to is class.)

TY. Cell phones away please. That means you, Mr. Simpson.

LUKE. I thought we weren't getting handouts anymore.

TY. Who told you that?

LUKE. It's just I heard it.

GWEN. We're supposed to be reading the book. Aren't we reading the book?

TY. Today we're discussing supplemental readings. Ms. Fletcher, perhaps you could read the first paragraph out loud for us.

ALICE. *(reading)* Some have been liberally educated, and all have lived in countries where the arts and sciences are cultivated to a considerable degree.

GWEN. Oh, brother.

ALICE. Misery is often the parent of the most affecting touches in poetry. – Among the blacks is misery enough, God knows, but no poetry.

TY. Thank you, Miss Fletcher. Would anyone like to comment on the supplemental reading? Miss Turner?

GWEN. Yeah, my comment is, I think this is supposed to be American history, so, I'd like to talk about that. And you know, my dad did call and complain that you were having us read crazy stuff so I don't think we should be talking about this handout.

TY. The author of this handout is Mr. Thomas Jefferson, one of our founding fathers, so I'm pretty sure we'll be able to squeeze this one by the school censors.

ERIK. *(laughing)* Check out this one: They are more ardent after their female: but love seems with them to be more an eager desire, than a tender delicate mixture of sentiment and sensation.

(Some snickers.)

ALICE. Wait a minute. "Nature by mental or physical disqualifications has marked infants and the weaker sex," so women are like babies, is that what he's saying?

TY. Do you think that's what he's saying?

GWEN. Okay. But we're still supposed to be reading the book. Like, if it's not in the book, I think we're not supposed to be reading it. Even if Thomas Jefferson wrote it. I mean, this isn't important, or it would be in the book.

ALICE. Thomas Jefferson wrote it.

GWEN. I don't care. It's not in the book.

TY. The author of all of today's selected readings was one of the great geniuses of his era, a Renaissance man, a titanic thinker and writer whose enormous contribution to Enlightenment – the idea of the rights of the individual – was built out of the lives of the more than six hundred slaves he owned during the course of his life.

GWEN. So?

TY. So does anyone have any thoughts about those facts, the way the facts come together. What does it make you think, about Thomas Jefferson?

ERIK. I think he was a president, and he's on the nickle.

ALICE. Plus he thought women shouldn't vote.

LUKE. Nobody back then thought women should vote.

TY. A lot of people did. Abigail Adams wrote letters to her husband –

GWEN. Are we going to have to read them, too?

ERIK. You mean we're doing to have to do MORE outside reading? In addition to the book?

TY. The Founding Fathers were particularly articulate letter writers. They wrote letters to everyone. Even when they hated each other, Jefferson and Adams carried on a lively correspondence.

LENNIE. Did he own slaves too?

TY. Adams, no, Adams did not. Jefferson, of course, yes. At one time he owned up to six hundred slaves.

GWEN. Okay but is like six hundred really a lot?

TY. He was the second largest slave owner in his county.

LUKE. Yeah but didn't they all own slaves?

TY. Franklin did, early in his life, but he was an abolitionist when he died. Alexander Hamilton, never.

ERIK. Who?

TY. Hamilton. He was – he's the guy on the ten dollar bill.

LUKE. So how come nobody talks about him? Jefferson only got a nickle and we have to spend a whole day on him.

GWEN. Plus he's not in the book.

TY. He and Jefferson apparently feuded relentlessly.

LENNIE. Why?

TY. Hamilton was a federalist and Jefferson felt that a strong federal government would prove a danger to the American people.

LENNIE. And he was right, right? Because that's what people are saying, right?

TY. What do you think?

ALICE. He had sex with one of his slaves.

TY. Excuse me?

ALICE. That's what I heard. That Jefferson had sex with a slave and she had his babies.

LUKE. So what if he did?

ALICE. *(angry)* So maybe she didn't want to have this asshole's babies!

TY. Maybe if we could stick with appropriate language, Miss Fletcher –

ALICE. Asshole isn't appropriate? Because he seems like a big asshole to me.

LUKE. No one could prove it.

ALICE. They can prove it now. There's this thing called "DNA." Ever heard of it?

LUKE. What is your problem?

GWEN. It's not in the book. None of this is anywhere in the book.

TY. Meaning what, Miss Turner?

GWEN. MEANING I know you don't think slavery was so great, because you would have been a slave? But like for us, like not all of us, but just my point is that's just the way things were then.

TY. I'm still not clear on your point.

GWEN. MY POINT IS of course everybody knows that slavery was bad! But that doesn't mean Jefferson was bad, that's what I'm saying! Alice. He had sex with one of his slaves.

LUKE. Everybody did!

ALICE. Everybody did not!

LUKE. People who had slaves did.

ALICE. Oh that makes it okay?

LUKE. It's not the same thing as killing babies.

ALICE. Fuck you.

TY. All right, Miss Fletcher –

ALICE. Fuck him! Men, they all think the same, I don't care that it was two hundred years ago, he was screwing one of his slaves, he was raping her –

LUKE. Oh that's crazy –

ALICE. If you can't say no it's rape!

LUKE. Feminist bullshit.

ALICE. *(fast, off handout)* "A tender mixture of sentiment and sensation," that's great coming from a fucking rapist!

LUKE. You can't call him a rapist.

ALICE. I can if he raped her.

LUKE. He was a founding father!

ALICE. Fucking rapist. FUCKING RAPIST.

TY. Class dismissed.

*(The class goes. **SONDRA** comes on, confronting **TY**.)*

SONDRA. Are you insane?

TY. It was a good class.

SONDRA. They told you no more handouts!

TY. That's not what they said.

SONDRA. It is what they said!

TY. They said no more radical thinkers. I didn't give them a radical thinker; I gave them Thomas Jefferson. No one can complain if I'm having those kids read Thomas Jefferson.

SONDRA. Ty, you are my big brother. I have looked up to you my whole life. So, you know that when I say this I mean it. You are a moron.

TY. I'm not.

SONDRA. One of your students called Jefferson a fucking rapist.

TY. I thought she had a pretty good point.

SONDRA. This is a recession! Teachers are getting fired all over the country.

TY. I'm not going to get fired. They need black teachers.

SONDRA. Have you been watching the news? People are mad. They don't want teachers, especially black teachers, especially black male teachers, telling their kids, telling them –

TY. Just because people are scared that doesn't mean that I stop teaching.

SONDRA. Don't talk to me like I'm one of your students.

TY. I'm a good teacher.

SONDRA. You're a moron. I'm calling Mom.

TY. Don't bother Mom.

SONDRA. She always said you were a first rate bonehead.

TY. She liked me better than you.

SONDRA. She won't now.

(*The phone rings. She looks at him. He answers it.*)

TY. Hello.

(*then*)

Yes, yes, Mrs. Loomis.

(**ALICE, JESUS, ARLENE** *and* **DON** *enter.* **ARLENE** *is cooking.* **ALICE** *is annoyed.*)

ARLENE. So what happened in this class?

ALICE. Nothing happened! We were discussing the Declaration of Independence.

JESUS. You were discussing more than that.

DON. According to some of the other parents you were discussing more than that.

ALICE. We were discussing Thomas Jefferson!

ARLENE. Was there a handout?

ALICE. There's handouts, Mom! We get handouts, it's school.

DON. Some of the other parents are concerned about some of the things this new teacher is having you read.

ALICE. It was all stuff by Thomas Jefferson.

ARLENE. I don't think you're telling us the whole story.

JESUS. That's an understatement.

ALICE. *(to* **JESUS**, *mad)* Stop it!

JESUS. Don't you think there are a few things you need to tell them?

ALICE. Such as WHAT?

JESUS. They're your parents.

ALICE. So?

JESUS. So, they love you. They are here to care for you, and guide you.

ALICE. You like them so much, you tell them.

ARLENE. Alice.

ALICE. *(annoyed)* WHAT.

ARLENE. What happened in that classroom?

   (pause)

   I got quite an earful from Marcia Turner. According to Gwen, you called Thomas Jefferson a 'rapist.'

DON. She did what?

ARLENE. She also used some very inappropriate language, apparently.

DON. More inappropriate than 'rapist?'

ARLENE. We're waiting.

ALICE. Waiting for what?

ARLENE. An explanation! This is the kind of behavior that gets you expelled, Alice!

ALICE. They're not going to expel me for calling Jefferson a rapist.

DON. Would you please stop saying that? That's appalling! Why would you say something like that?

ALICE. Because he did, he – he –

ARLENE. Is this what they're teaching now?

DON. Is this what this new teacher is teaching them? That's what's going on down there now, we have some liberal – black – teacher –

ALICE. No, he didn't –

DON. Well, where would you get such an idea?

(**ALICE** *looks at them. She looks at* **JESUS**. *He nods to her.*)

ALICE. I was just, I got, I was upset. Cause I know someone, I know, there's this person I know, this girl, who is, she thinks she maybe is pregnant. And she, it's because she went with this guy who had sex with her and she didn't, he didn't even ask he just did it. And I was thinking about that, Jefferson had, you know, the story is about him and his slave –

DON. That's never been proved.

ALICE. They have DNA.

DON. DNA doesn't prove anything.

ALICE. It does, Dad, on CSI, and Criminal Minds, and Law and Order –

DON. That's different.

ALICE. It's not different! DNA is a fact!

ARLENE. I don't understand what this has to do with what happened in school today.

ALICE. Well, because – okay. I was thinking about that slave, and how she couldn't say no and then she had all these babies. And you don't know, maybe she didn't want to.

'Cause I know my friend, she definitely doesn't want to. She just, she doesn't, she didn't want to have sex with this guy and now she's supposed to have a baby? So that's what I was thinking.

ARLENE. Who is this girl.

ALICE. I can't tell you.

ARLENE. Is it Betty? Or Gwen?

ALICE. *(loud, fast)* I'M NOT TELLING YOU MOM DON'T GUESS.

DON. Don't you raise your voice to your mother!

ALICE. THEN STOP YELLING AT ME!

JESUS. Arlene, Don! Arlene! May I? Let's just take a moment and pray.

(He goes to them and takes their hands.)

JESUS. This has been a hard day, heavenly father. Arlene and Don are good Christians. They've raised their daughter well. She is a good and obedient girl, she gets good grades, she never talks back.

ARLENE. Praise you, Jesus.

JESUS. Thank you, Arlene. Let them take strength from the knowledge that I am here with them, and will guide them as they guide her. Amen.

ARLENE. Amen.

DON. Amen.

JESUS. All right. Here we go. Arlene! Let Alice know you love her, and you only want to help.

ARLENE. Well of course I just want to help!

ALICE. You do?

ARLENE. Absolutely.

ALICE. How?

ARLENE. Well, teen pregnancy is hard, honey. Your friend – and I don't need you to tell me her name right now, I know these situations are delicate, and you can just wait to tell me when you're more comfortable – but she should be seeing a counselor, and a doctor. Has she told her parents yet?

ALICE. No.

ARLENE. Well, she needs to do that.

ALICE. She's scared to.

DON. *(to* ARLENE*)* Listen. I'm not so sure I like her hanging out with some pregnant – girl.

JESUS. Don.

DON. I mean it.

ARLENE. Has she talked to a priest?

ALICE. Why would she talk to a priest?

ARLENE. Well, if she is afraid to talk to her parents, she needs to talk to someone who will counsel her and help her make the best choices for herself and her baby.

ALICE. She doesn't want to have the baby.

(then)

She's not going to have the baby. She's definitely not having the baby.

ARLENE. Oh.

ALICE. She's having an abortion.

ARLENE. Well, she can't actually do that, without her parents consent, so if they don't know about it, yet, that's something she will need to think about.

ALICE. I don't know about that, but she's definitely having an abortion.

DON. Okay –

ARLENE. Don.

ALICE. She was practically raped. It was like date rape, kind of? That's what it sounds like to me.

DON. I don't want you talking to this girl.

ARLENE. Don, Alice is clearly trying to be a good friend to someone.

DON. Someone who could even think about that, that she could kill a baby? Killers do not deserve our friendship. And she needs to know that. You need to know that. I don't want you talking to this girl.

JESUS. Don, maybe we could pray about this.

DON. Sure, I'll pray. I'll pray for the soul of that baby.

(JESUS *takes his hand.*)

DON. Jesus.

JESUS. Yes, Don.

DON. Please help my daughter understand that people who want to kill innocent children are evil.

JESUS. They're baby killers, and God's vengeance will rain down on them, his fury will smite them, and they will be consigned to the eternal flames.

DON. That's right.

JESUS. Damnation without end.

DON. Oh Lord!

JESUS. Unending pain and suffering be theirs almighty father, forever and ever –

DON. Praise you Jesus –

JESUS. The sword of righteousness will come down upon her head –

ALICE. *(loud)* What are you doing?

JESUS. We're praying.

ALICE. You're crazy. All of you are CRAZY.

(*She goes.* **SIMON** *comes on, with* **PRODUCTION ASSISTANTS** *helping him with his mikes.*)

SIMON. Today's guest – let me tell you something. I have been trying for YEARS to get this man to agree to come on the show. So you can imagine how thrilled I am today to announce a rare, rare appearance from one of the greatest – some would say THE greatest – founding fathers: Thomas Jefferson!

(**JEFFERSON** *approaches, in a spotlight. He bows, formal. Thunderous applause.* **SIMON** *shows him to a chair.*)

SIMON. I cannot tell you how thrilled we are to have you, Mr. Jefferson. Can I call you Tom?

THOMAS JEFFERSON. I prefer Thomas.

SIMON. Of course you do. Let me ask you to share with our viewers, Thomas, why you decided to join us today, to break your silence as it were, after so many years.

THOMAS JEFFERSON. I felt there was some confusion.

SIMON. I can't disagree with you there! People, today, what is going on in government is so far a field from your intent, we know that! That is what we are objecting to! Our point – and we make it over and over and over again – is what was the intent. What did YOU believe you were setting in place. When you created America. Tell us, Mr. Jefferson. Lay it on me.

THOMAS JEFFERSON. First of all: The federal government should have been murdered in it's infancy.

SIMON. I could not agree with you more on that one.

THOMAS JEFFERSON. It was Hamilton's obsession. A dangerous pretender at all times, a man with a complete lack of character, a galling arrogance built entirely on the myth of military ability. Duplicitous to the core, every moment of his life was spent trying to undo what we had accomplished.

SIMON. Who is this?

THOMAS JEFFERSON. Hamilton. Alexander –

SIMON. Alexander Hamilton, right right, the guy on the ten dollar bill! Which due respect you got to ask: how did he get the ten dollar bill and you only got the nickle? Cause that doesn't seem right.

THOMAS JEFFERSON. He invented the treasury.

SIMON. Horrible. Now you had a real problem with debt yourself, didn't you. Monticello was always in debt, I read that once.

THOMAS JEFFERSON. These history books are distortions!

SIMON. But you were a big reader, weren't you? I took a tour of Monticello once. What a beautiful place. Books everywhere. You were a terrific egghead, they told us. Sitting up there on the top of the hill, the king of your own paradise.

THOMAS JEFFERSON. Not the "king," please.

SIMON. No no don't be modest! That place is like a palace, and the grounds are so laid out, with the different levels of slave quarters, the house slaves are right next door – and they had very nice accommodations.

THOMAS JEFFERSON. It was my duty to treat them well. We revisited the question constantly. The country was not ready for emancipation. It placed a responsibility on the owner, to provide and care for these unfortunate people.

SIMON. Which you did but they had to work too! People today, I'm telling you, we have these Mexicans and Africans and Arabs, people who mean us harm are thronging to our shores, coming across our borders, eating our food, going to our schools, taking our health care and and we're expected to pay them a living wage. On top of that! Oh don't get me started on the minimum wage insanity, it's ruining business. Corporations don't want to be here!

THOMAS JEFFERSON. Americans should work the land. The gentleman farmer is my idea.

SIMON. A nation of farmers! I like that. Cause the farms now, you know who runs them? Illegal immigrants! Taking jobs away from Americans, who need them! Now that didn't happen in your time, did it?

THOMAS JEFFERSON. No. We used slaves.

SIMON. But they were legal slaves! And like you said, you took care of them. Now let me ask you something, I've wanted to ask one of you guys this for a long time: When you said "all men are created equal," you really meant all MEN, right? You meant to leave women out. That wasn't a mistake.

THOMAS JEFFERSON. Women and infants don't have the capacity to reason. They cannot participate in government, they are under the care of government.

SIMON. That's what I say! Everyone's all, let's go back, let's be strict constructionists, which I agree, I absolutely

agree we should go back to how this nation began –
because you and your friends were just geniuses, it's
clear that you guys really knew what you were doing –
and you didn't leave women out because it sounded
better, "all men are created equal" just SOUNDS better
than "all men and women are created equal" but that's
not why, that's not why you left them out! Is it!

THOMAS JEFFERSON. Thomas Aquinas once noted that
'As regards to nature, women are defective and
misbegotten.'

SIMON. *(roaring)* I love that! Cause let me tell you something
Tom, these women nowadays, its a nightmare, all you
hear are 'my rights,' 'you insulted my rights,' God you
want to kill yourself, you guys really had the right idea.
All MEN are created equal, not women, and we're
talking WHITE men. Cause that's the way it should be.
And let me tell you something, my viewers? That's the
way they want it. You're phenomenal.

(Lights shift. **LINDA** *and* **BRENDA**, *in* **LINDA***'s kitchen.
They have been watching* **SIMON**. **BRENDA** *is drinking
a bottle of wine, while* **LINDA** *cooks.)*

LINDA. Turn him off.

BRENDA. Oh he was making a joke.

LINDA. Well, it's not funny. They don't have to act like it's
all 'ha ha hilarious' because it's not.

BRENDA. Listen to you Miss Feminist. Did Marcia call you
about this new thing that happened with the history
teacher?

LINDA. She left a message but she drives me crazy so I did
not call her back.

BRENDA. But listen to this, this new history teacher, he gave
out another one of those handouts and they all got
into a big argument apparently and Alice Fletcher
apparently got a bit worked up and she called Jefferson
a 'fucking rapist.'

LINDA. You're kidding.

BRENDA. I am not kidding.

(*She snickers.* **LINDA** *laughs with her.*)

LINDA. Alice Fletcher!

BRENDA. I know, I always thought she was such a quiet girl.

LINDA. Me too! I like her. And you know Lennie has such a crush on her. But you are not allowed to tell anyone I said that.

BRENDA. Has he asked her out?

LINDA. Oh please. He's still, but he did go out for that talent show, because she's always in it.

BRENDA. Oh that's right.

LINDA. I thought he was really good, but he's still upset because he just messed up a few of the words. They're so sensitive at this age. I said to him, 'no one noticed!' But of course I'm just his mother, he doesn't believe a word out of my mouth.

BRENDA. Well. It was pretty surprising, he didn't know the words to the song.

LINDA. He didn't – it wasn't that bad.

BRENDA. Yeah, but its not like people didn't notice.

LINDA. It was just a few words!

BRENDA. It was a few words in the national anthem.

LINDA. 'O Beautiful' is not the national anthem.

BRENDA. Don't get mad at me. I'm just telling you what happened. Hey Brian.

(**BRIAN** *enters, with a case.*)

BRIAN. Hey, Brenda. Hey honey.

(*He kisses her.*)

LINDA. You're early.

BRIAN. I had a half day.

LINDA. You had a half day? You didn't tell me.

BRIAN. (*playful*) Well I don't tell you everything.

LINDA. Well why don't you tell me everything?

BRIAN. Because maybe you don't need to know everything. What's for dinner?

(He goes and gets himself a beer. She looks at the case.)

LINDA. Maybe I'll tell you what's for dinner when you tell me what you've been doing all afternoon. What's this?

(She flips the case open as he reenters. Her playful tone immediately evaporates.)

LINDA. Oh good Lord. Oh for heaven's sake.

BRIAN. Now, just hang on.

LINDA. You brought another gun into this house. After I told you –

BRIAN. This is my house too, Linda, in fact I am the one who paid for this house and maybe you don't get to tell me what I am and am not allowed to do in it!

(There is an awkward pause.)

BRENDA. You know what? I got to get home, Eric has got to be wondering where I am. I'll see you, Linda. Good to see you, Brian.

*(She goes. **LINDA** and **BRIAN** square off.)*

LINDA. I thought I was clear how I felt about this.

BRIAN. You told me how you felt and I told you how I felt. And I have some agreement with you, a larger weapon is not appropriate inside the home and so I removed that, I did as you asked and secured it in a safe place outside the home. But the reality of our daily lives is that bullets are flying on our streets.

LINDA. Bullets are flying, have you gone nuts?

BRIAN. No I have not!

LINDA. There are no bullets flying –

BRIAN. There are and there will continue to be. And we have to take personal responsibility for our security and allowing citizens to arm themselves in self-defense is the only, the only reasonable course of action here.

LINDA. Course of action! What are you talking about? Brian, what on earth, what on earth.

BRIAN. Things are happening, Linda.

LINDA. What's happening is my husband's gone crazy, that's what's happening.

BRIAN. I can't talk to you.

(He starts to go.)

LINDA. Wait, wait! Come on, Brian. You can't just blow in and out of here like this. You have to – oh lord. Things are happening. I can see that. Why don't you, what is it?

(He looks at her. There is an unhappy pause as he struggles to talk.)

BRIAN. I understand your being afraid.

LINDA. I'm not afraid.

BRIAN. You're afraid of the guns. I understand that. But if you leave them, if you put them in boxes and lock them up, then what use are they? If something happens. They're no use at all.

LINDA. Nothing's going to happen.

BRIAN. You don't know that!

LINDA. Brian. We live in a nice house on a nice street in a nice town. People are starting to act a little weird because – well I don't know why, because people on the television are saying some crazy stuff. But other than that –

BRIAN. What if it's not crazy? What they're saying on t.v.?

LINDA. You mean you really think something bad is going to happen? Like what?

(He sits, bewildered.)

BRIAN. I don't know. I just…You don't know, because you're here all day. And I want you to be here, you and Lennie, it makes me feel – safe – to know that you're all right, and you're here. Because out there – everyone is so angry. I've never seen people so angry.

LINDA. What are they angry about?

BRIAN. I can't even say! It doesn't matter even, what it is. It's like everybody knows something is wrong, and it might just suddenly be wrong for you. That's the feeling. That the world is about to explode. That everything we worked for will vanish. Not vanish. Be stolen. Or burned. That our cities will burn. Invasion, there are invaders already here, it's happening, or it's already happened. You're being robbed. Not that you've been robbed, but that you're being, and you have to be you have to stop it, somehow. It's on you to stop it but it's already happened. I don't know. I don't know! That someone is going to come into your house and take it. That nothing's safe. None of us are safe, anymore. And if you don't, if I don't – do – something – it will all be lost. Lost.

LINDA. But it's not like one thing?

BRIAN. It's everything.

(He shakes his head. She goes to him.)

LINDA. Sweetheart. You have to stop torturing yourself. We've already been through lots of hard things and we're all right. That time you had to have your knee surgery and you couldn't work for five months and they tried to fire you instead of paying the workman's comp and we had to hire that horrible lawyer who charged us too much and then they tried to take the house –

BRIAN. Oh god –

LINDA. I know it was awful but we got through it and you got your job back and it was fun, honestly –

BRIAN. It wasn't fun.

LINDA. Having you around the house that whole time was fun. That's mostly what I remember, the horrible parts just kind of disappear and the rest was – I mean it wasn't always fun you got so cranky and the only thing that would calm you down was Ben and Jerry's ice cream.

BRIAN. Chunky monkey.

LINDA. That's right. Chunky monkey saved the day. I swear this whole family is just all about food. So I don't, I just don't think anything horrible is going to happen to us, and even if it did, I wouldn't care because we have each other. The only thing that scares me is losing you or Lennie, and when you go away, into your head like that, that's what it feels like, it feels like I lost you.

BRIAN. You haven't lost me.

LINDA. Don't go away like that. I hate it. I just hate it when you won't talk to me.

BRIAN. We're talking now.

LINDA. Yes we are, and it's better already. Now come on.

BRIAN. Where are we going?

LINDA. We're going down to the Key Foods and get some Chunky Monkey.

(She takes him by the hand. They kiss. Then they go.)

*(Lights on **LENNIE**.)*

LENNIE. Your brain is so weird. Like, you're thinking something and then you feel something and you totally forget what you were thinking in the fist place. And then you remember it again like the next day, like where did that go, and then why did it come back? Are the things you think real, even, if they can disappear like that? Because there's you and there's your brain and then there's the thing your brain thinks and if you wrote it down before you forgot it, it would be outside of you, like on a piece of paper. So it would be real then, but not if you don't write it down? Because writing is just writing, it's not the thing you're writing about, those are two different things. I like thinking about questions, my brain is happy when it thinks things. So you would think I mean I would think that because you're happy your brain would want to stay there and just stay happy but then it's like this other part of you comes along and just wrecks everything.

And it's like IN you, like IN your brain but then you know, like, really, it's like you're having an argument with yourself and there's a couple of people in there. But that's, okay look that's totally, I'm not saying you're like a multiple personality or anything; that's not what I'm talking about. Although I would like to meet someone with multiple personalities, that sounds kind of interesting to me. Unless some of them were mean to the other ones. That wouldn't be so good. To have a mean person in SIDE you? Because when people are mean that really is what makes the ideas – that make you happy – it makes them disappear.

(The high school students appear, as a wall.)

LUKE. Hey it's the little fag.

GWEN. O beautiful! You think you're beautiful, fag?

ERIK. He's a talented travesty.

LUKE. O beautiful, for naked thighs.

*(**LENNIE** tries to push by them. **GWEN** stops him. **ALICE** and **JESUS** appear behind.)*

GWEN. Where you going?

LENNIE. I'm going home. Can I please –

GWEN. 'Can I please, can I please?'

LENNIE. I'm just trying –

GWEN. 'I'm just trying…'

LENNIE. God! This is –

GWEN. This is WHAT? THIS IS WHAT?

LENNIE. Nothing –

GWEN. This is America, is what it is! This isn't some fag country, that people can just make fun of! This is America!

LENNIE. God –

(He tries to push by her. She shoves him. He shoves her back. The two guys leap at this.)

GWEN. What the fuck –

LUKE. What the fuck are you doing –

ERIK. Fuck you, you little fag –

(**LENNIE** *lands on the ground.* **ERIK** *kicks him.*)

ALICE. *(overlap)* Stop it! Stop it! STOP IT. What is the matter with you?

(*She and* **JESUS** *go to* **LENNIE.** *She glares at* **LUKE.**)

LUKE. What's the matter with ME?

GWEN. Forget it. They're not worth it.

(*She pushes* **LUKE** *to follow her. He does.* **ERIK** *goes with them. Ashamed,* **LENNIE** *stands, brushes her off.*)

LENNIE. I'm okay, I'm okay!

(*He starts to pick up his books.*)

ALICE. You're not okay! Have you reported this?

LENNIE. Reported?

ALICE. Yeah, to like a teacher or something.

LENNIE. What are they going to do about it?

ALICE. Well, they could stop you from getting tortured.

LENNIE. Look, could you not, it's fine.

ALICE. It's not fine.

LENNIE. Just stay out of it okay? It's my own fault.

ALICE. How is this your fault?

LENNIE. You were there! You saw it! Everyone saw it!

ALICE. You mean that song? At the talent show? Yeah, okay, that was stupid but that doesn't mean they're allowed to do this to you.

LENNIE. It's okay.

ALICE. It was a stupid talent show. No one gives a shit about it except for like you know. Freshmen and theater losers. Why did you even do it?

LENNIE. My mom told me to.

(*There is a terrible pause.*)

ALICE. You did it because your *mom* told you to?

(*He starts to cry.*)

ALICE. Oh. I'm sorry. I'm sorry.

LENNIE. It's okay.

ALICE. They'll forget about it.

LENNIE. Sure.

ALICE. You should tell a teacher. Seriously. You should tell somebody.

LENNIE. Yeah sure.

(*She goes.* **JESUS** *watches* **LENNIE** *for a moment.*)

ALICE. Are you coming? Not you. Jesus.

LENNIE. Oh.

ALICE. (*to* **JESUS**) Come on!

(*She goes off.* **JESUS** *follows her. A moment of silence.* **LENNIE** *arrives home.*)

LENNIE. Mom?

(*He looks around.*)

Mom?

(*He sits at the kitchen table. He cries for a long moment. He stands. He looks at the box on the table. He opens it. He stares at what is inside. He takes the gun out. He holds it. He puts it to his head.*)

(*Blackout*)

(*Sound of a gunshot*)

End of Act One

ACT TWO

*(***LENNIE***'s funeral. A casket. Everyone, surrounding it, wears black. Several people carry umbrellas.)*

MINISTER. Since the children have flesh and blood he too shared in their humanity so that by his death he might destroy him who holds the power of death – that is, the devil – and free those who all their lives were held in slavery by their fear of death. The book of Hebrews tells us, not to fear death as Christ did not fear death. We pray that our son Leonard is at rest, O lord, with the angels, by your side. In the name of the father, the son and the holy spirit.

ALL. *(mumbling)* Amen. Amen. Amen.

*(Silence. All the mourners start to drift away. ***LINDA*** suddenly turns.)*

LINDA. No. NO. No no no no no –

*(She throws herself on the casket and weeps as if her heart would break. The other mourners continue to drift away. ***BRIAN*** goes to her. ***JESUS*** and ***LENNIE*** are revealed, watching.)*

BRIAN. Come on, sweetheart. We have to go.

LINDA. No, no, you can't, they can't. Oh god. My little boy. I can't, I can't leave him here.

*(***JESUS*** goes to her.)*

JESUS. Come on. It's okay. He'll be okay.

LINDA. Will he?

JESUS. Come on.

*(***JESUS*** and ***BRIAN*** help her stand and move off. ***LENNIE*** is left alone, watching. ***ST. PAUL*** enters, with a clipboard. He looks at it, looks at ***LENNIE***.)*

ST. PAUL. Boy did you fuck up.

LENNIE. It was a mistake!

ST. PAUL. I'll say. Suicide is a big big no no. Not a lot of confusion around this one. Mortal sin pretty much defines it. You're going to hell, and pronto.

(He starts filling in forms on his clipboard. **ST. AMBROSE** *hurries on. He carries his head.)*

ST. AMBROSE. Wait! Wait – St. Paul, St. Paul, excuse me sir. We've been asked to wait for a moment.

ST. PAUL. By whom.

ST. AMBROSE. I don't know.

(He goes. **ST. PAUL** *sighs.)*

LENNIE. You're not St. Peter?

ST. PAUL. *(annoyed)* No, I'm St. Paul, which would be why he called me "St. Paul."

LENNIE. I thought St. Peter was the one who met you, when when –

ST. PAUL. When you commit suicide?

LENNIE. It was an accident!

ST. PAUL. Do you want to see the video?

LENNIE. No I don't want to see the video –

ST. PAUL. Because it doesn't look so accidental, what you did. You picked the gun up, pointed it at your head –

LENNIE. I know what I did! I know, I know what I did.

(He sits, depressed.)

ST. PAUL. Stupid.

LENNIE. I know it was stupid!

ST. PAUL. Eternal damnation. That's what happens to suicides.

LENNIE. Look, could I talk to someone else?

ST. PAUL. Like who, St. "Peter?" St. Peter, everyone wants to talk to St. Peter and his big fluffy beard. "You are Peter and upon this rock I will build my church." He never actually said that, you know. The whole idea of a church, that was *my* idea. Jesus didn't want to start a church, it never even occurred to him, he was the one through whom we have received grace and apostleship to bring about the obedience of faith for the sake of his name among all the nations, including you who are called to belong to Jesus Christ, but he wasn't exactly pragmatic. Everything was love and forgiveness and compassion. And by the way, by the way even if he did say it? "You are Peter and upon this *rock*?" Peter didn't exactly follow through, did he? The Bishop of Rome. He never even went to Rome! The Catholic church wasn't even es*tab*lished until three hundred years later! These things take vision, you can't just sit around drinking wine and *praying*. Well, I'm not waiting. Here, we have a lot of paperwork to get through.

(He hands him the clipboard. **JOAN OF ARC** *enters. She wears armor, carries a sword. It might be nice if she were smoldering, a little. She starts to yell and berate* **ST. PAUL,** *in French.)*

ST. PAUL. Oh for crying out loud. Here she goes.

(She continues to yell in French.)

Could you please stop yelling at me, I am in charge here. They burned you at the stake for a reason. Oh for crying out loud. Anybody got a match? I am just doing my job!

(She is now gesturing to him, to go, as she continues to berate him in French.)

Fine. Fine! YOU do it then. Only I warn you, it's complicated. He's a suicide! Got that? Not a martyr. He did it to himself. He's going to hell, see? I already checked it off.

(He shows her the place on the forms. She starts to yell at him again. He goes.)

(A moment of silence as she looks at the clipboard. **LENNIE** *looks at her.)*

ST. JOAN. *(French accent)* That guy's an asshole. He always thinks he is in charge. They are all like that, when someone says this is power, you have power. They think it means they know something. But power does not mean that. Power has many meanings. Rarely does it mean knowledge.

(**JESUS** *enters, quickly.* **JOAN** *looks at him and starts to complain to him in French, about* **PAUL**.)

JESUS. I know, I know.

(She continues to speak, explaining what he was about to do concerning **LENNIE**. *She hands him the clipboard.)*

Yes, yes, thank you. I can take it from here. Thanks.

(She nods and stomps off.)

I'm sorry I'm late. Your mother is really upset.

(**LENNIE** *looks at him and starts to cry.)*

LENNIE. I'm sorry.

JESUS. I know.

LENNIE. I didn't mean to.

JESUS. I know.

LENNIE. Is she going to be okay?

JESUS. No. She's not going to be okay, ever again.

(**JESUS** *puts his arm around him and they go off.)*

(**LINDA***'s kitchen.* **BRENDA**, *and* **ARLENE** *are there, taking care of her.)*

(She sits at the table.)

ARLENE. Oh you brought your seven layer bars! I could just kill you! You are just going to wreck my diet.

BRENDA. I know but they're Linda's favorite.

ARLENE. Look how nice yours come out. I tried making them once for a Christmas party, they just fell apart.

BRENDA. Did you put the evaporated milk on last?

ARLENE. Yes that's what I did; I did that!

BRENDA. No no, you put half of the evaporated milk on at the beginning, right over the graham crackers. Spray the pan with Pam, and mix the graham cracker crumbs with the butter in a separate bowl and then put in half the evaporated milk, and then put the other half of the can on top, at the end.

ARLENE. Ohhhh. I didn't do that.

BRENDA. And you always have to use real graham crackers. Don't buy the can of crumbs they sell in the grocery store. You have to take real crackers and crumble them yourself.

ARLENE. You want one of Brenda's seven layer bars, Linda? She make them better than anyone.

(**LINDA** *doesn't respond to this.*)

BRENDA. I'm gonna make some coffee. No. You know what I'm going to make? Tea.

ARLENE. That sounds good. You want a cup of tea, sweetheart?

(**LINDA** *starts to cry.*)

BRENDA. Oh honey.

ARLENE. You have to try now, Linda. I know it's hard. But you need to turn to the Lord and ask him to give you strength. He never sends us more than we can bear. For yea though I walk through the valley of the shadow of death I will not fear, for the Lord is by my side.

BRENDA. Arlene, maybe now isn't the best time.

ARLENE. Her faith is the only thing that is going to get her through this. She knows that.

LINDA. He sent this?

ARLENE. What's that, honey?

LINDA. You just said God sent this.

ARLENE. I don't think I said that.

LINDA. *(angry)* You said he never sends us more than we can bear, that means he sent this. So you think God did this, God told Lennie to to to –

ARLENE. *(overlap)* No no no –

BRENDA. *(overlap)* That's not what she said at all, Linda –

ARLENE. *(overlap)* Linda, you know that's not what –

LINDA. God wanted my son to shoot himself in the head! Is that what you're saying?

BRENDA. *(clear)* Linda. You know that's not what she meant. What happened is a terrible tragedy and Arlene's just trying to make you feel better, the best way she knows how.

ARLENE. I just think that if we prayed together.

BRENDA. Shut up, Arlene. You just shut up now. *(then)* I'm going to turn on the TV. We're all going to have a cup of tea and eat a cookie and watch some television, how does that sound?

ARLENE. I think that sounds great.

BRENDA. Me too.

(**BRENDA** *finds the clicker and turns on the television.* **SIMON** *comes on.* **JOHN ADAMS** *sits next to him.*)

SIMON. Tonight's guest – let me tell you something, this is a guy who knows everything there is to know about a subject that is on everyone's mind these days and that is: Revolution! Mr. John Adams, welcome to the show.

JOHN ADAMS. Thank you.

BRENDA. Where do they get these guys?

JOHN ADAMS. I'm very pleased to be here.

ARLENE. I don't know but I think it's so cute. Did you see when he had Thomas Jefferson on?

SIMON. John let's jump right in to the heart of this thing. It's become clear to a lot of my viewers, all my viewers honestly, I just hear this over and over – that this country has reached an impasse much like the one you found yourself in.

JOHN ADAMS. You have an insane British monarch trying to inflict his will onto the American people?

SIMON. It's worse than that actually. It's our own federal government!

JOHN ADAMS. Well, I was a federalist from the start but it was Hamilton who really insisted on things like a standing army, a national bank –

SIMON. Disaster! The federal government is a complete disaster!

JOHN ADAMS. All Hamilton. Even the constitution, I don't think that was his idea but the things he did to push it through were reprehensible, I hated the man.

SIMON. So do my viewers! Because we, we the people, of the United States of America, we want the federal government to leave us alone! Leave our rights in place! Because the thing – the thing that you know, and I know, makes revolution possible – is the right to bear arms. You couldn't have done it, right? If someone had taken your guns away?

(LINDA *stands up.*)

BRENDA. I'm turning this off.

LINDA. Leave it on.

SIMON. How could you have even had a revolution without the right to bear arms.

JOHN ADAMS. Well, we didn't have any rights at the time.

SIMON. But you did have guns.

JOHN ADAMS. Of course.

SIMON. Because let me tell you something. This is what's happened to America. Liberals are trying to take our guns. And they're using any excuse. This week the excuse is – and this is a tragedy – some teenager in Delaware shot himself.

BRENDA. Linda honey don't do this to yourself.

(LINDA *silences her with a gesture.*)

SIMON. This young man, unstable, gay apparently, commits an unspeakable act. Our sympathy goes out to his family. A horrible horrible tragedy. But you know what the liberals are saying about it?

JOHN ADAMS. "Liberals?"

SIMON. Don't ask, you don't want to know. The liberals are saying this tragedy means we have to get the guns out of the home.

JOHN ADAMS. But then how would you defend yourselves against the indians?

SIMON. Right? It makes no rational sense. A crazy teenager shoots himself in the head so we should get the guns out of the hands of the people!

LINDA. He wasn't crazy. He was perfect.

BRENDA. Linda.

JOHN ADAMS. No free man shall ever be debarred from the use of arms.

LINDA. He came home nobody was here and Brian left it here because we were having a fight.

SIMON. Did you say that?

JOHN ADAMS. No. Patrick Henry.

LINDA. We were fighting about because I didn't understand it.

SIMON. The right to bear weapons is the right to be free. You must've said that one.

JOHN ADAMS. I don't know who said that one.

LINDA. – why everyone is so angry all the time and then Brian had bought a gun one that was too big and then he said he wanted one in the house and I was upset.

BRENDA. Linda –

SIMON. To disarm the people is the best and most effectual way to enslave them.

JOHN ADAMS. Don't know that one either.

LINDA. – because I never we didn't have them I know people say they grew up with them but we didn't –

SIMON. *(droning overlap)* But let's move on to the subject of militias. Because having a federal army, that didn't mean that you wanted to do away with state militias.

JOHN ADAMS. Certainly not. People felt very strongly about that.

LINDA. And I wasn't here, the gun was here and I wasn't HERE.

SIMON. Do you hear that everybody? The founding fathers WANTED us to form our own militias. God wants it.

BRENDA. Sweetie, sweetie –

LINDA. I'm always here! It's the best moment of my day, when he comes home from school.

SIMON. And resistance to tyranny is obedience to god. You said that, right?

JOHN ADAMS. That was Jefferson.

SIMON. You know this one? "Resistance is futile." No, sorry, that's the Borg.

*(He laughs. **JOHN ADAMS** chuckles, to be polite.)*

LINDA. Why wasn't I here.

*(The sound goes off. **BRENDA** holds **LINDA** while in silence **SIMON** and **JOHN ADAMS** laugh at their own jokes.)*

*(**ALICE** and **JESUS** arriving to class with the other students, and the founding fathers. Everyone is very quiet. **TY** starts to hand out pieces of paper.)*

ERIK. *(unnerved)* What is this?

GWEN. Another handout?

TY. It's a couple of excerpts about the history of voluntary death in western culture. Also known as suicide.

LUKE. Oh brother.

TY. You have an opinion you want to share with the class about today's handout, Mr. Simpson?

(A pause.)

LUKE. No.

*(There is a moment of silence as **TY** continues to pass out the pages. He hands one to **GWEN** and moves on. She shoves it off her desk.)*

TY. There is a simple summary at the top of today's handout, who would like to read it? Erik?

ERIK. Suicide is an act of a human being intentionally causing his or her own death.

GWEN. Look. This is a history class. What does suicide have to do with American history?

TY. Would anyone like to answer that?

GWEN. It wasn't a real question!

TY. Then how about we keep reading. Erik?

ERIK. Over one million people commit suicide every year. The world health organization estimates that it is the thirteenth leading cause of death worldwide.

GWEN. Why are we reading this?

TY. Because one of your classmates took his own life, Miss Turner.

GWEN. I am well aware! We are all well aware!

TY. And since this is a history class, I thought it might help us, as we struggle to make sense of this seemingly senseless act, by putting it first in a historical context.

(*He nods to* **ERIK.**)

ERIK. The Abrahmic religions consider suicide an offense toward God due to a religious belief in the sanctity of life. Conversely, during the Samurai era in Japan –

(**GWEN** *stands, sudden.*)

GWEN. You guys all want us to talk about this? Then let's talk. What Lennie did was stupid and a sin, and he's going to hell now.

TY. That is certainly the view of many cultures.

GWEN. No. That's the truth! And that's all there is and I want a history class! I want to talk about Pilgrims and the Boston massacre and and and the American Revolution and and I want to memorize the preamble to the constitution and that's it! This is crap what you teach. It's just junk! What are you, a moron? We don't want to talk, we don't want to think! I want to learn what I'm supposed to learn, take a multiple choice test and go home!

ALICE. I want to talk about it.

GWEN. Then go to the guidance counselor!

TY. I want to talk about it too. He was one of my students. I'm upset. I want to talk about it.

JESUS. I want to talk about it.

GWEN. You don't get a vote!

ALICE. Why not, why doesn't he?

TY. America is supposed to be about a free exchange of ideas.

GWEN. What kind of free exchange of ideas can you have about suicide? The Bible says don't do it! HE said don't do it!

JESUS. I never did, actually.

GWEN. You know what? I don't care if you did or didn't. No one cares ,what you actually said. No one gives a shit.

(The kids erupt at this. All the following lines overlap.)

ALICE. Look you don't have to be so nasty about –

GWEN. I don't need to talk to you either –

ERIK. I want to talk about it. I don't see why we shouldn't talk about it.

LUKE. Nobody told him to kill himself.

GWEN. Which is what I've been saying all along!

JESUS. When a person is in despair it's a situation that I think everyone should be concerned about and my sense is.

ERIK. All I'm saying is I think was sad, I don't think it was stupid –

GWEN. I don't care! I don't think we should have to be all boo hoo because its his fault not mine.

LUKE. Nobody told him to kill himself. And the Bible says its a sin.

(They start to yell at each other.)

TY. One at a time ONE AT A TIME.

ALICE. He was being bullied.

(This lands in the silence. A beat.)

TY. What?

ALICE. Lennie. I told him to come talk to you. Not you specifically, but a teacher. Anybody. They were torturing him.

TY. Who was?

ALICE. Gwen. Erik. Luke.

LUKE. That's nuts.

TY. Be quiet. Alice! This is a very serious accusation.

ALICE. It's true. Ever since the talent show, when he just, he just messed up the song and they kept, it was horrible, the things they said to him.

TY. You witnessed it? What were they saying?

GWEN. Who gives a shit? Just because you say something to a person that doesn't mean it's your fault if he does something stupid and kills himself! He was crazy. He killed himself because that's what crazy people do.

ALICE. They called him a fag and they said he hated America. They yelled at him a lot and I think they were texting him and then they started beating him up.

LUKE. That's nuts.

ALICE. It's not nuts I SAW IT.

TY. All three of you come with me.

LUKE. We didn't do anything!

TY. The rest of you, I want a five hundred word essay on the free exchange of ideas. You three, with me, NOW. Alice, you too.

*(He takes **LUKE**, **ERIK**, **GWEN** and **ALICE** off. The others stare at each other.)*

JESUS. Can I borrow a pen?

(Lights shift.)

*(**TY** is alone in the gym, dribbling a ball. He sits in silence for a moment. **ALICE** approaches.)*

ALICE. Hi.

TY. Yes, hello, Miss Fletcher.

(She sits next to him. There is a moment of silence.)

That was very brave, what you did. I appreciate your coming forward.

ALICE. It was brave what you did.

TY. How so.

ALICE. Well…people are going to be mad at you. For getting the police involved.

TY. Bullying is nothing we can take lightly anymore. I think that's obvious. I just…wish he had come to me. Before things got so bad.

ALICE. I told him to. I did, I told him to.

TY. I'm sure you did.

ALICE. *(starting to cry)* I wish, I wish – I wish –

TY. You did what you could.

ALICE. No. I didn't. Oh god. Oh, Jesus.

(JESUS enters, goes to her.)

JESUS. Alice? It's all right, Alice.

ALICE. It's not all right.

(He holds her.)

He was here. He was in trouble. And I didn't, I just told him he was stupid –

TY. You told him –

ALICE. Not in a mean way, I was nice, I told him he was stupid in a nice way but then I just left. He was in trouble and I didn't and I should have, I should talked to him but I was too fucked up because I'm pregnant and it wasn't my fault this idiot raped me and now I'm pregnant and I'm just I'm really messed up about it because there's no one I can talk to about it except Jesus and he is no help, no help at all.

JESUS. I'm trying!

ALICE. Not hard enough!

JESUS. A lot has been going on, there's a lot of people in trouble around here right now!

ALICE. Stop making excuses.

JESUS. I'm not! Come on. Let's pray.

ALICE. I don't want to pray! I want some answers! I can't have a baby! There is no reason for me to do that and I am not GOING to do that and if none of you will help me I will take care of it myself!

TY. Hang on. Hang on.

ALICE. I AM NOT KIDDING HERE. I need help. I need HELP.

(**SONDRA** *appears, in her kitchen.*)

SONDRA. You got to be kidding me.

TY. She came to me for help.

SONDRA. Ty I am telling you right now you are brain dead.

TY. Just talk to her.

SONDRA. I am not talking to her!

TY. (*to* **ALICE**) My sister is a social worker. She has a lot of information about abortion, and what your options are.

SONDRA. She is underage. She needs to talk to her parents.

ALICE. I CAN'T talk to my parents.

SONDRA. Sweetheart, you have to, because you have no rights in this situation.

ALICE. I had no rights when that idiot raped me, either! So how did this happen, how did I end up with no rights? This is America. Everyone keeps saying on TV, 'Ooh, they're taking away our rights, we have a right to fight for our rights and that and they're trying to take it away' well I don't have a right to anything anyway so why is this such a great country, huh? How is this so great? Everybody has a right to guns, everybody has a right to kill people but I don't have a right to to myself? All this shit about free, we're all so FREE and they're taking away my FREEDOMS. What are my freedoms. Just because I'm a girl I have no freedoms?

(*silence*)

TY. Who raped you.

ALICE. Oh please! I was in the back seat of his car, I went back there with him because I thought he was cool! So I didn't have the right to say no! And I certainly don't have the right to bring charges. What do you think THAT would look like? If I even tried? I don't even have the right to talk about this. I tried to talk to my parents I DID and they WOULDN'T. Girls don't even have the right to talk in this stupid country.

SONDRA. Oh, boy.

TY. If we don't help her, who will?

SONDRA. She is white teenage girl, Ty! You are a black teacher. A black man, who is her teacher. If it gets out you helped her get an abortion, what you think is going to happen to you?

JESUS. Can I say something?

SONDRA. No you cannot. What are you even doing here?

JESUS. I'm Jesus.

SONDRA. I know who you are. I asked, what are you doing here?

JESUS. Sister, don't you be starting on me. I have been holding hands with these girls for two thousand years and I don't need attitude from you on who belongs in this conversation. Uh huh you heard me. I'm talking to you now and lemme ask you this one, if this were a black child we're talking to, boy out there treated her bad, left her in this condition, her mama and daddy ain't gonna help her, that's a whole different matter, isn't it? This child needs help. It don't matter to me the color of her skin. She's come to you for help.

SONDRA. You're okay with this?

ALICE. If you read the New Testament –

SONDRA. Yes, I have read it –

ALICE. Well, he never said anything about it. Mostly all he talks about is love, compassion, be nice to each other –

JESUS. No judgement.

ALICE. No judgement, things like that.

(*They consider each other.*)

SONDRA. How far along are you, honey?

ALICE. Five weeks.

TY. Can we help her?

SONDRA. If we get her to Connecticut. She has to talk to a counselor, answer some questions. But there's no parental consent law. *(She sighs.)* Let me call a friend of mine, works in a clinic up there.

(She pulls out her cell. Lights shifts. **TY,** **SONDRA,** **ALICE** *and* **JESUS** *on a road trip. All of them have Big Gulps.* **JESUS** *is looking at a road map.)*

JESUS. Well, we could take 278 across Staten Island, shoot up the BQE to the Whitestone, and then we're practically there, if the traffic's not wretched.

SONDRA. How likely is that.

JESUS. I realize, but the only other reasonable option is taking the turnpike all the way up to the GW Bridge and picking up the Sawmill to the Cross County to the Hutch and that will be just as bad if not worse. Ugh. New York is a nightmare, even when you're just trying to get around it.

SONDRA. I would imagine you'd do a lot of business in New York.

JESUS. Oh honey I'm tired just thinking about it.

ALICE. Why do you do that?

JESUS. Do what?

ALICE. Well, you kind of – you know, you end up sounding like whoever you're talking to.

JESUS. Oh I don't do that. You do that.

ALICE. No I don't.

JESUS. I don't mean you. I mean people do that. You know this. People, they think I'm whoever they want me to be. Which is them. So I just, I sound like them.

TY. Okay, hang on.

JESUS. No, it's true. I'm whoever people want me to be. I really have no control over it.

ALICE. Well, it's kind of annoying.

JESUS. Oh my god, I'm so aware. There are these guys, they all live together in a house in Washington, and they pray all the time and all they pray about is cheating the American people and how much money they can walk away with, and all of them are complete, they're cheating on their wives! Seriously one affair after another and they're all "JESUS loves you brother. JESUS loves your sin. JESUS is with you." And I'm like, Oh, yes I do! I love your sin! Meanwhile I'm thinking I never said that. I said: Give to the poor. Have some compassion. I certainly never said be mean to gay people. Please. I love gay people! I'm so sorry that they feel sad, so much of the time. Because really, they have good hearts. And they're so much fun at a party.

TY. Well why don't you tell people that?

JESUS. Nobody listens to me. They hear what they want to hear.

SONDRA. Maybe you could talk louder.

JESUS. People are already talking so loudly. I didn't want to contribute to the noise.

SONDRA. They need to hear from you! Who you are! Why is that so difficult?

ALICE. Seriously we are all really confused. It would help so much if you would just be yourself.

JESUS. Nobody wants that. Everytime I bring up the poor and the meek people just ignore it. And seriously that was really important to me. It is important!

ALICE. That's good. Help the poor. That's good. What else you got.

JESUS. Let's see. It was something to do with all sentient beings coming to enlightenment.

TY. No, that was Buddha.

JESUS. It was like that, though! Compassion. The energy of the universe is compassion. Time is compassionate.

TY. Yes.

JESUS. The Kingdom of Heaven. Is here. Yes, that's right. It's right here. A road trip.

TY. The kingdom of heaven?

JESUS. Yes. It's us. It's all of us. The kingdom of heaven is at hand. *(beat)* Can we stop at the next gas station? I have to pee.

SONDRA. We just stopped fifteen minutes ago!

JESUS. I know I know.

SONDRA. I should never have let you buy those big gulps.

*(She keeps driving. **LINDA** at home, in the kitchen. **LINDA** is holding something in her hand. **BRIAN** enters.)*

BRIAN. Hey honey. How you doing, sweetheart.

(She doesn't answer. He looks around.)

So what's for dinner?

(It lands like a lame joke. She doesn't react.)

Come on, honey. You're not going to send me down to the diner again. Their meatloaf just isn't that good. *(beat)* Linda, come on. You have to try. Just a little. If you just try a little bit every day it will get better. I promise. Why don't you come with me. You got to at least eat, honey. We'll go down to the diner and stay away from the meatloaf. Have the chicken and rice.

LINDA. That was his favorite. Three cans of soup. *(then)* You go. I can't stand to look at you.

BRIAN. Linda, please. He was my son, too.

LINDA. You don't get to call him that anymore. He was not your son. He was MY SON and you MURDERED HIM. He was NOT YOUR SON.

*(She goes. **TY** enters on a run. **MRS. LOOMIS** enters behind him.)*

MRS LOOMIS. Mr Janilaris! Do you have a minute?

TY. Right now? Sorry, I got stuck in traffic, and I'm late for my first period.

MRS LOOMIS. It doesn't have to be right now. Just sometime today. Stop by my office, when you have a minute.

TY. I have classes back to back until noon, should I come by then?

MRS LOOMIS. That will be fine.

TY. Is everything all right?

MRS LOOMIS. What do you think?

(**SIMON**, *on television.*)

SIMON. My friends – I have never been so completely convinced – ever – that we are on the right path. The way is long, but through our toiling and our courage, we find ourselves on the brink of our own salvation. Our faithfulness to each other, and to the truth – the truth of America, what is, what it was always meant to be – has brought us here. I'm so excited today, friends. I tell you I'm on fire with happiness. Because this is how we get to where we're going. And tonight we continue our series of interviews with the founding fathers with the ever-fascinating Benjamin Franklin.

BEN FRANKLIN. Yes, how do you do.

SIMON. What an honor it is to have you, Mr. Franklin.

BEN FRANKLIN. Well, I don't know if I'm honored to be here. Yet.

SIMON. There's that famous wit.

BEN FRANKLIN. Was that witty?

SIMON. Let's reacquaint our viewers with a few of your minor achievements. The Declaration of Independence. The constitutional congress. The acts of confederation.

BEN FRANKLIN. The invention of electricity, that's my favorite one.

SIMON. What a man. What a resume! It's mindboggling, the things you titans racked up almost incidentally while you went about forming this great nation. Creating a set of ideals that would be strong enough to sustain us all through time and trial. We need you to share with us, Mr. Franklin. What you and the other founders intended has never been more important to this great nation.

BEN FRANKLIN. Now that actually is why I'm here. Because I really did want to get this one bit straight for you. The fact is: We had no intent. This is so surprising that you all think we had some singular intent. We had debate, is what we had. For instance, I've been watching what is going on here, in your town this week, and just to be very clear, when we debated the right to bear arms we most certainly did not mean a child blowing out his own brains. If you think that's what we meant you've misunderstood us entirely.

SIMON. Oh – oh no. We don't endorse suicide.

BEN FRANKLIN. But you do continue to encourage people to arm themselves, people who don't know how to be deliberate and circumspect with a weapon!

SIMON. Our god given right to bear arms –

BEN FRANKLIN. God doesn't create rights. We create rights. And if the citizenry abuse them, their leadership can take them away!

SIMON. Then you are advocating the repeal of the second amendment?

BEN FRANKLIN. I am advocating temperate debate, and common sense.

SIMON. These are not temperate or sensible times!

BEN FRANKLIN. Every time has it's challenges, don't talk to me about challenging times.

SIMON. That's right! The tree of liberty must be watered, well, and often, with the blood of tyrants!

BEN FRANKLIN. Yes that's another one. You have to stop saying that and you know why? Because you don't have any tyrants! We had George the Third! You have many honorable men and women who are valiantly struggling to make this omnibus of a government we created work!

SIMON. Not all of them are honorable, Mr. Franklin. I'm sorry to have to tell you: Many of them are not honorable at all.

BEN FRANKLIN. You can say that about anybody, at any time. For instance, when you used that terrible tragedy, the young man shooting himself, as an excuse to sell more of your guns I didn't think that was very honorable.

SIMON. I wasn't –

BEN FRANKLIN. Oh yes you were; of course you were. Do you mind if I ask, do you own a gun manufacturing enterprise?

SIMON. Oh – no no, it's a part ownership –

BEN FRANKLIN. That's what I thought. Where were we?

SIMON. Honorable men and women.

BEN FRANKLIN. All are sinners; some are saints. Few are one or the other.

SIMON. But you valiant few, our founding fathers –

BEN FRANKLIN. Yes I know you would love us to be your saints, for you, I hear what you say about us, it's really nonsense. You use us! You invoke a misbegotten version of us as heroes and saints, and then you use that image of the past to justify your own lack of compassion. Oh, the things you would justify in our name!

SIMON. What are you saying?

BEN FRANKLIN. You know what I'm saying. We were no better than you, stop acting like we had all the answers! Some of us behaved in really unforgivable ways. You know what bothered me, was the way they all went after Hamilton. It was disgraceful. Such a passionate and brave and truly brilliant statesmen, from the humblest beginnings. You know what Adams called him? A "base born brat of a Scots peddler." And at least he said it! Jefferson and Burr, they all were thinking it.

SIMON. Let's get back to the example you set. The country you made. The ideals!

BEN FRANKLIN. But that's why Hamilton was so important. He put in place everything, the articles of the federation, the treasury, the navy, the national debt –

SIMON. And for that alone he should be hung.

BEN FRANKLIN. The fact is this country would never have even survived without his passion and his very real genius. And they drove him to suicide.

SIMON. Now now I'm going to have to correct you, Mr. Franklin.

BEN FRANKLIN. Bold.

SIMON. Yes it is but I do know my history. Alexander Hamilton died honorably. In a duel.

BEN FRANKLIN. He didn't discharge his weapon. He shot for the trees. He stood there and let Burr murder him. It was a suicide.

SIMON. We'll have to agree to disagree.

BEN FRANKLIN. There's an idea. You might try that with each other. You might try creating your own world. With each other. That's what we did.

*(**MRS**. **LOOMIS** steps forward, with a clipboard and shouts.)*

MRS LOOMIS. Now I'm going to call this meeting to order.

(Everyone starts to gather.)

SIMON. The American Town Hall! A tradition that goes back all the way to pre-revolutionary times! The moment when the entire community comes together to air it's differences and clarify it's meanings. Who are we individually? Who are we as a people? Ladies and gentlemen – it is my privilege to bring to you live from the Selbyville High School Auditorium a special edition of the Simon Williams Show on Democracy as we live it!

*(Everyone starts to shout. **MRS**. **LOOMIS** tries to yell above them.)*

MRS LOOMIS. Yes yes yes PLEASE – *(louder)* YOU WILL ALL HAVE YOUR MOMENT TO BE HEARD BUT YOU ARE GOING TO HAVE TO WAIT UNTIL I CALL ON YOU OR IT IS JUST GOING TO BE – oh Jesus.

*(Everyone keeps shouting. A loud whistle blows. **JESUS** steps forward with a microphone.)*

JESUS. Everyone will get a turn. For a moment I'd like to lead us all in prayer.

(He prays.)

Please let us remember we are a community of beings who share this earth with each other. Let us listen to each other with grace and humility. Amen.

*(***MRS. LOOMIS*** *takes over.)*

MRS LOOMIS. THANK YOU. THANK YOU JESUS for those good words. Now I know, it has come to the attention of the school board that a lot of people are upset about some recent events that have occurred in the high school.

This has been a difficult time for our community and a lot of people have asked for a public forum, so that we can have a chance to air our differences and discuss the procedures the school administration has adopted –

MARCIA. There were no procedures. There were NO procedures. Our children were expelled and handed over to the police without so much as a courtesy call to the parents!

(The parents rumble in assent.)

MRS LOOMIS. That is not what happened –

BRENDA. That is exactly what happened! We have been exposed in the most horrendous way to the judgement of –

JOE. *(overlap)* Our kids are being condemned in the press, the press is having a field day with this! People are calling them murderers! On the street, on the television!

BRENDA. People are spitting at us! The internet, people are calling for the death penalty! All on the word of one teacher –

MARCIA. That teacher had it in for them from the beginning. He had an agenda. It wasn't good enough for him to just teach the book.

JOE. He had an axe to grind. And now he's grinding it on our kids's heads.

(More chaos. **JESUS** *blows his whistle.)*

MRS LOOMIS. Thank you, Jesus. As I said, this is a tremendously complicated and upsetting situation and we need to preserve some order. Everyone will have a chance to speak. But since so many questions revolve around accusations which were made recently, concerning alleged bullying which allegedly contributed to the alleged suicide of student Leonard Ryan –

(The noise level threatens to rise again but **MRS. LOOMIS** *squashes it.)*

– that is where we'll start. First we will hear from Mr. Janilaris, who will explain the events in which he participated which led to the schools actions, uh, regarding the alleged bullying which allegedly led to the alleged suicide.

(She looks around for **TY,** *spots him. He approaches.* **JESUS** *hands him the microphone.)*

TY. Thank you, Mrs. Loomis.

(silence)

I would like to say that I have real sympathy for everyone involved in this crisis and I hope we can all listen to each other.

(Someone hisses. **TY** *takes a breath and continues.)*

After the tragedy, when Lennie shot himself, I was told by one of his classmates, Alice Fletcher, that she had witnessed an incident of bullying which involved three fellow students. She saw them verbally harassing Lennie and physically attacking him, shortly before he took his life. I had no choice but to bring that information to the authorities.

(several people, shouting)

MARCIA. You had no evidence!

ERIK. *(overlap)* No one even asked us –

LUKE. *(overlap)* The whole thing is a lie –

JOE. *(overlap)* There was no grounds! As Americans we have a right – these are our children!

TY. *(overlap)* It was my responsibility as a teacher to take these accusations seriously.

MRS LOOMIS. One at a time, please!

GWEN. He had it in for us! He was teaching all kind of crazy things and I went and told my parents that it was junk and he's mad, they told him that he couldn't just teach whatever he wanted and now he's taking it out on us!

(There is a pause.)

MRS LOOMIS. Mr. Janilaris do you want to answer that?

TY. *(startled)* Are you – are you kidding?

(then)

That's absurd. I don't have anything to say to that. It's ridiculous.

GWEN. He wasn't teaching a real class. He was just trying to teach propaganda and he should be fired.

ERIK. A lot of people had trouble in that class. It was like crazy the stuff he wanted us to read, there were all these handouts.

MARCIA. And when we raised it with the administration we were shot down! No one wanted to know!

TY. We are not here to talk about the curriculum.

MRS LOOMIS. We are here to talk about everything. This is a community. Everyone will be heard.

*(**TY** looks at her, pissed. She does not look at him. More shouting. **LUKE** finally is the loudest.)*

JOE. It's not only that! I don't like what was being taught and I do think that we have the right to say what you can and cannot teach our kids, I agree with that. But that's not even the whole picture. The whole picture I see, is that there is no evidence.
To make these accusations, to have our children arrested – to take them out of the school and take them

to the police and have them arrested for something, even if they did do it, it doesn't amount to anything, but then to say oh, I'm going to do this with no evidence whatsoever, that is absolutely unacceptable and we should sue the school if you ask me. For letting him do this.

(People applaud.)

This is exactly the sort of thing that we object to. Turning this country into a police state. Our kids were taken from us and their rights were stomped on. This is our country, and you cannot treat us like this. Because I am standing here and telling you we will not allow it.

MRS LOOMIS. Thank you Mr. Simpson. Mrs. Turner?

MARCIA. I agree with Joe. My daughter is a good student and when I heard what she did? It was nothing! Kids say things to each other, it's just what happens in high school! But now they're not even allowed to say things to each other without the police getting involved?

BRENDA. I thought that too. It was kids being kids. I'm not saying it's right, I told Eric I was really unhappy with some of the stuff I had heard, that he did, but –

MARCIA. It's all hearsay! People exaggerate!

JOE. There's no evidence! There was never any evidence!

(People start to argue.)

TY. That's not true. Excuse me – excuse me –

(JESUS *blows his whistle. Everybody shuts up.)*

I would like to respond to some of these remarks.

MRS LOOMIS. Certainly.

TY. It's untrue that there was "no evidence." There was a witness. We have the testimony of a fellow student who witnessed the acts of bullying. Which is increasingly seen as a crime in our culture. It was my responsibility to report what the student witnessed.

JOE. By "this student," you mean this girl, the girl who said she saw something?

TY. *(testy)* Yes, that is what "witness" would mean.

JOE. Because my son has something to say about that. She's not as innocent as she looks.

DON. What is that supposed to mean?

JOE. It means I don't know why we're taking the word of one girl, who maybe has reason to lie.

DON. My daughter is not a liar!

TY. There is no reason to believe Miss Fletcher would lie about what she saw.

MARCIA. There is every reason to believe it because my daughter says that she didn't do it! And Luke and Erik, they deny it as well! So it's her word against theirs, why would the word of one girl count more than three?

TY. The police found her credible.

BRENDA. The police should never have been involved!

TY. But they were involved because a crime happened!

BRENDA. There was no crime! If it was anything it was kids being kids, my kid is a good kid!

JOE. That girl lied! My son has testimony! She lied to get him in trouble! Give me that microphone, my son has testimony.

(**MRS. LOOMIS** *takes the microphone from whoever has it at this point and gives it to* **LUKE.** **LUKE** *steps forward, awkward and defiant, speaks into the microphone.*)

LUKE. Okay the thing is…we, like, I went out with Alice. It was just once but it went you know, further, than maybe it should have and we had sexual relations. And then I realized, I'm involved with someone else and that was an important thing for me, so I told her, Alice, that I didn't want to see her anymore. Which made her mad.

TY. I fail to see how this is relevant.

LUKE. Well, I'm telling you. I mean, I do regret that we went as far as we did, sexually, but it was seriously just the one time and that was a mistake but then she was all, which is why, you know, when she was calling Thomas Jefferson a rapist in class? All I'm saying is that's what that was.

TY. Yes I remember that you took offense to her calling Jefferson a rapist.

LUKE. Well who wouldn't.

TY. But you had a particular sensitivity to it.

LUKE. So?

MRS LOOMIS. Do we need to revisit this particular episode, Mr. Janilaris? Is it relevant?

TY. I don't know if it's relevant or not. I remember it made me wonder, at the time, why he would be so sensitive to that particular word. Rapist.

ALICE. Stop it! Stop it! It doesn't matter. Stop it.

LUKE. What did you tell him?

ALICE. I didn't tell him anything!

*(Everyone stares at her. She sits back down. **ARLENE** looks at her, worried.)*

JOE. What my son is trying to say is that she has a lot of problems. There's a lot more to this story.

MRS LOOMIS. Miss Fletcher.

ALICE. What.

MRS LOOMIS. Do you want to say something?

ALICE. No.

LUKE. Whatever she says she is lying.

JOE. It's true. He told me all about it. She had a crush on him –

ALICE. That's not, it's not –

JOE. But he had another girl he was seeing so she made the whole thing up.

ALICE. *(snapping)* That isn't what happened!

MRS LOOMIS. Could you please pass the microphone to Alice? I think we all need to hear her side of whatever this is. Please.

*(**LUKE** hands her the microphone. **ALICE** looks at it, speaks into it.)*

ALICE. I'm – what am I supposed to tell them?

*(She looks around for **JESUS**.)*

JESUS. Just tell them the truth, sweetheart.

JOE. They want to put my son in jail because of what you said!

TY. About Lennie. What you said about Lennie.

JOE. We want to know why you would lie about that!

ALICE. What I said is what happened. I saw them yelling at Lennie and saying horrible things. And then they tried to beat him up. I saw it.

LUKE. She's mad because she got pregnant and now she's trying to take some kind of crazy revenge. That's all this is!

BRENDA. She's pregnant?

MARCIA. I knew there was more to this.

JOE. She got pregnant and when he said he was with another girl she went crazy.

ALICE. That's not – no! That's not – what happened. It's not.

(Everyone stares at her. A pause.)

MRS LOOMIS. Are you pregnant, Miss Fletcher?

TY. She does not have to answer that! She is not on trial here!

MRS LOOMIS. These are very serious accusations and the parents of your classmates have a right to get to the bottom of what has happened here. Is he telling the truth? Did you have sexual relations?

(A pause.)

ALICE. I –

JOE. It's a simple question!

MRS LOOMIS. Please.

ARLENE. I don't – think this is appropriate. My daughter is a good girl. It was hard for her, to come forward and tell what she saw. You should not be punishing her for that. Your kids are in trouble, I see that and I'm sorry about that. But a boy is dead, and we need to respect that and we need to pray –

BRENDA. I am sorry about what happened too but sending my son to jail is not going to bring him back!

JOE. She has not yet answered the question. Are you pregnant?

(He glares at her.)

ALICE. No. I'm not.

LUKE. Bullshit you're not.

ALICE. I'm not. I'm not pregnant.

LUKE. You told me you were! Were you lying then, or are you lying now?

ALICE. I'm not lying. And I wasn't lying.

LUKE. One of them is a lie! You're a liar!

ALICE. No. I was pregnant. And I'm not pregnant anymore.

(There is a silence.)

I took care of it. You, it wasn't sexual relations, it's crazy to call it that. I told him to stop and he didn't. And then I was pregnant and I did tell him that because it was, and he, nobody, I couldn't tell anybody because nobody would help me. And so then someone finally helped me and I got an abortion and I'm not pregnant anymore and that's the truth. And I did see what I saw. I saw them hurting Lennie. Hurting him because they thought it was funny. They made fun of him because he forgot the words to that song that he sang at the assembly and – I was so screwed up I couldn't help him. I couldn't help him.

(She is crying. **JESUS** *goes to her and holds her hand.)*

So I wanted to help him now.

(She dries her eyes. Silence.)

ARLENE. You – Alice, you –

ALICE. I'm sorry, Mom. I'm sorry, Daddy. I didn't want you to know.

LUKE. You had an abortion?

ALICE. What do you care?

LUKE. That's disgusting.

DON. Who helped you? *(beat)* WHO HELPED YOU?

(He stands, at his seat, but doesn't move to her.)

DON. She said somebody helped her. I want to know who did that.

ALICE. Who helped me?

DON. Who helped you commit murder? Who "helped you." Kill your own child.

ALICE. That's not what happened.

DON. You just said it was.

TY. Please. This is so unfair to her –

DON. You stay out of this. She's not your child.

TY. This is just – a private matter –

DON. What do you know about it?

TY. I just want Alice to be protected.

DON. Or maybe you want yourself to be protected.

TY. No.

DON. No? You know what? I don't believe you! Ever since you got here, seems to me you're involved in everything that happens around here. What are you teaching in that fucking history class? Suicide, murder, abortion –

ALICE. He didn't do it! I did it myself. I found out I went on line and found out that you could get an abortion without parental consent in Connecticut so I found a clinic and I went to Connecticut on the bus and I went by myself. He's my teacher for crying out loud. He didn't do anything. He doesn't have anything to do with any of this.

DON. You went to him before. To make your crazy accusations.

ALICE. They weren't crazy!

JOE. Weren't they?

ALICE. No. No! He helped me!

JOE. Helped you how?

ALICE. For Lennie. He helped me and Lennie –

JOE. Helped you lie about Lennie –

ALICE. I wouldn't lie about that!

JOE. But you'd lie about other things.

ALICE. I didn't. I wouldn't.

DON. Wouldn't you? Seems to me you'd do just about anything. I don't know who you are.

ALICE. I'm – me. Dad. I'm… I didn't want to have a baby. He raped me. And I didn't want to have a baby.

DON. I don't believe a word out of your mouth.

(She looks at him. Silence. When she speaks she is very strong and clear.)

ALICE. See, I knew that. I knew everybody would think that. And that no one would help me.

DON. But someone did. Who was it?

(A pause.)

ALICE. *(then)* It was Jesus. I prayed and prayed and Jesus came. He talked to me, and he told me it was all right, and that I would be all right, and that he loved me. And he told me I had rights too. And that the kingdom of heaven is at hand. And he helped me get an abortion. That's what I meant when I said someone helped me. It was Jesus.

(A beat.)

JOE. *(to room)* All right. I think we're done here. You all heard her. She talked to Jesus, who helped her get an abortion. If anyone thinks her testimony will stand up in court? I'm willing to take my chances with that. Come on, Luke.

MRS LOOMIS. I have to say, I'm inclined to agree with you, Mr. Simpson. Thank you, everyone for your input tonight. I will alert the authorities as to the new information we acquired this evening and I feel confident that the charges will be dropped. The suspensions as well. We will expect to see all of you in school tomorrow.

LINDA. Can I say something?

(She raises her hand.)

BRIAN. Sweetheart.

LINDA. I want to say something.

(She steps forward. There is an object in her hand.)

BRENDA. Linda. Listen to me. We are so sorry about what happened to Lennie. But there is no evidence that our kids are involved. This girl is not a good witness. She is confused, she is in a lot of trouble, and there's no evidence. You have to let go of this.

*(**LINDA** fumbles with the object in her hand. The words of the bullying texts flash behind them, large. FAGGOT. FUCK YOU. FRUIT. YOU SMELL. I WANT TO PISS ON YOU. YOU'RE UGLY. WHY DON'T YOU DIE?)*

LINDA. This is Lennie's cell phone. It was in his pocket. When I came home and found him. There are things on it. They were sending him. Words. Attacks. My little boy. Who would do something like this?

(The words continue to flash. FUCKING ASSHOLE. DIE. WHY DON'T YOU DIE. FRUIT.)

BRENDA. Those are – that's not admissable in court.

LINDA. Who cares? WHO CARES? Why are you acting like this? You know it happened. Your children are monsters. My child is gone. He is no longer on this earth. And this girl – she said no. To a baby. That is the country we've created. A country unfit for children. A place where children cannot be born.

(then)

At night I tell myself that we are all together, through time, the dead and the living. That we share creation with our ghosts. And sometimes that is enough. But mostly I just want to see my son again. I want to teach him to be a man. And that will never happen now.

(She looks at the cell phone.)

Is there a way to delete this stuff? Take it off the phone, so it's not there anymore? I don't want to see this anymore.

(A pause.)

JESUS. I can do it.

LINDA. Would you?

JESUS. I'm not actually very technical? But I can try.

(He steps forward and takes the cell phone from her. Starts to delete the messages.)

LINDA. Thank you.

*(The meeting drifts away, revealing **LENNIE** and **ALEXANDER HAMILTON**. **LENNIE** watches **JESUS** and **LINDA** delete the texts from his cell phone.)*

LENNIE. My mom is so sad.

HAMILTON. Well, suicide. You know it the minute you pull it off. What a colossal mistake.

LENNIE. I thought you died in a duel.

HAMILTON. You bought that? That I lost? To Burr? Please. I let him shoot me.

LENNIE. Why?

HAMILTON. Oh, you know I was depressed.

(He sets up a chess board and a couple of chairs for them.)

HAMILTON. I created America. And then they threw me aside! My pride was wounded. I was angry. Emotions. They make you forget things that really you should remember.

*(**JOAN OF ARC** enters carrying a baby.)*

ST. JOAN. What a gorgeous girl! Oo la la, c'est magnifique, le petite femme. Ah, chess! I love this game.

LENNIE. I never learned.

ST. JOAN. Then I will teach you. I am really good at this game.

HAMILTON. You start with a pawn.

ST. JOAN. And then right away, right away, you bring out the queen.

HAMILTON. You always want to do that.

ST. JOAN. It's a surprise, strategy is all about surprise.

HAMILTON. Only it's not a surprise if you always do it.

(JOAN *starts to lecture him in French.*)

English, please, oh god I hate it when you do this –

(*As they argue,* LENNIE *drifts away, watches his mother. She leans into* JESUS, *exhausted.*)

LENNIE. Mom?

(LINDA *looks up.*)

Mom?

(*She listens.* JESUS *listens. Blackout.*)

End of Play

www.ingramcontent.com/pod-product-compliance
Lightning Source LLC
Chambersburg PA
CBHW070643120726
47909CB00004B/1557